THE VERY GENIUS NOTEBOOKS

THE VERY GENIUS NOTEBOOKS

THE CHRONICLES OF DELTOVIA

Olivia Jaimes

Andrews McMeel
PUBLISHING®

September 7th

You're holding in your hands something big. Something amazing. Something critically important to the history of the world and art.

Unless you're listening to the audiobook version of this book, or somebody is reading it to you. Or maybe you're reading it, but you've got it propped up somehow so it's not actually in your hands at this exact moment. It's fine if this is you, just please update that first sentence in your head for accuracy.

FOR EXAMPLE:

I am listening to something important

OR PERHAPS:

I'm looking at a book propped up in front of me, and I'm really, honestly, I gotta say, loving it

You're holding the book where me and my friends made our name as geniuses. Where we crafted the greatest story the world has ever seen, but just hasn't seen yet:

the CHRONICLES of DELTOVIA

I told my mom I was working on a new masterpiece with my friends, and she said, "Oh? Is it a sequel to *The Candelabra*?"

This was a very low blow, and a sign that my mother does not understand my genius. It's not a surprise, really. For some reason, people don't seem to realize quite how much of a genius I am. I think it's because they don't know the signs and because I am so humble.

SIGNS OF A CREATIVE GENIUS:

Hair messy but in a genius way

Deep in thought

This backpack is not a sign of my genius, I just like it

The Candelabra was my first attempt at writing a book, and I made several key mistakes with it. First of all, I wrote it chapter by chapter on the internet, instead of in a note-book like this one, which meant that my mom could find it before it was done and show it to her friends.

Wow, Misha! You did a *really* *good job!*

(Mom's friend)

I was also, let's just say, *younger* when I wrote *The Cande-labra*, which meant I included some lines that at the time

I thought sounded cool, but which I now understand are horrible and corny. There are times when I'm just walking around, minding my own business, when I remember a line from *The Candelabra* and just:

It is true suffering. But it is this suffering that is going to make *this* book so much more DEEP and artistic.

And that's not the only thing that's different this time around. I wrote *The Candelabra* alone, which—while of course I *could* have finished it, if I'd wanted to—meant that my friends would have been left behind if I became famous from it and would definitely have missed me when I was a celebrity.

So it was actually a really good thing I only finished three and a half chapters of *The Candelabra*, because now I can write

with June and Ollie, and we can all become millionaires together.

I truly believe there's a good chance that "June, Misha, and Ollie" will be household names by the time you're reading this. I told this to June, and she was like,

It takes a lot of time, effort, and luck to become famous, Misha. Few who attempt it succeed. We could try our absolute hardest and still fail. There's no guarantee that the world is going to spare an ounce of attention for us. I put our odds of becoming celebrities at 80%.

Then I told Ollie, and she was like,

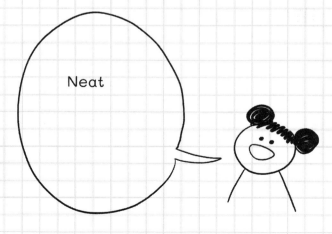

Neat

I told my mom that we were going to be very famous very soon, and she just laughed and quoted *The Candelabra* at me, and then made me take out the trash.

MISUNDERSTOOD

Well, "a true heart's true wish always comes true"

I, for one, have no doubts. We know all the secrets of writing, like character design and cliffhangers. We'll succeed because our hard work and talent will make our book so undeniably good that the world will have to take notice of us. And also because destiny.

Not the cheesy kind of destiny I wrote about in *The Candelabra*:

You are destined to be a Heart Princess who brings JOY to all the people

Actual destiny. Cosmic destiny.

You might say we have a reputation for being different at Lakeview Middle. Sure, we aren't what you'd call "popular," but it's not like that's ever mattered to us. We've known we were different for a long time now:

"Mysterious"　　　"Intense"　　　　　　　"Captain" of the "Lacrosse Team"

These are all simply signs of an extremely obvious truth: we're meant for something bigger than normal life at this school. There is a celestial fate out there for us, mysterious and unknowable and impossible to pin down.

It's this book. We're going to write it here.

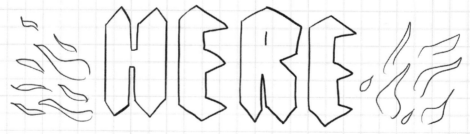

(Not literally here. On some of the next pages.)

Of course, if you're reading this, you've probably been a fan of our work for some time. It makes sense. I'm fully expecting to get a sequel, a movie, a TV show spin-off of the movie, a reboot of the movie, and at least one behind-the-scenes documentary out of our story. You might be reading this in a museum somewhere, or maybe you paid a lot of money for the original copy to add to your collection.

YOU(?)

Jeeves is holding the book for me, and I'm really, honestly, I gotta say, loving it

But just in case you somehow have picked this up without knowing the lore of

yet, allow me to introduce you to this great and epic world that my friends and I have carefully crafted through our years of friendship:

THE CHRONICLES OF DELTOVIA
is the story of a group of friends who are all normal middle schoolers until one day a mysterious mirror appears in their cafeteria surrounded by fog and enigma and they walk through it and emerge in a dark and gritty magical world where everyone has transformed into a magical version of themselves and they all have powerful psychic elemental powers now.

That's as far as we've gotten. But with a start like that, I'm thinking we're pretty much set. It should be smooth sailing from here, especially since we've each worked hard to make our own characters for the world.

Mine is *Melodia*, a middle schooler with a mysterious past. When she emerges on the other side of the mirror, she discovers that she has psychic lightning powers and a single demon bat wing. Her goal is to survive in Deltovia while uncovering the dark secrets of her past and the tragic origins of her single wing.

She looks like this:

June and Ollie have characters, too:

June's character is named *Jayana*.

Ollie's character is named *Ollie*.

They'll introduce themselves here soon. We're all going to be adding to the story in this book as we get inspired. That's what this notebook is for: creating a tale that will change the world, as a team.

I have a plan to get it published, too. There's a girl in our class with a famous mom who's written a book and been on TV at least twice. If we just get this notebook into her hands and ask her to get it published, she'll see how brilliant it is and, well........

September 8th

Dear Misha,

In the future, please do not throw this notebook at my head like a Frisbee.

Please hand it to me.

If you do throw it at my head, please say, "Hey June!" loud enough to be heard over the sound of classes changing and make sure we have made eye contact first.

ACCEPTABLE   UNACCEPTABLE

Here you go

Thank you

Kicking

Frisbee

This →

Sincerely,
June

Dear Misha (again),

I'm writing again to make sure my tone didn't come across as too upset in my last note. Reading it over, I realize it may have come across harsher than I wanted. If it did, I'm very sorry. Please accept my sincerest apologies. I would have erased it and written something else except I wrote it in pen.

Your friend,
June

Dear Reader in the Future,

This is June. You may have read Misha's introduction to this book and thought we were not serious about writing this book. You might have thought that because Misha thinks it will be "smooth sailing" that we are underestimating the challenges of writing a novel.

Let me assure you that I understand exactly how hard it will be for us to write a book. It may take us years, even decades. We may die before we finish it. We may lose touch with our families and loved ones and withdraw from society, all because we are hopelessly trying to finish our book.

But I'm willing to sacrifice everything for it because I truly believe we can create a very good world together, and also because Misha needs me to look out for her, and without me the project may fail totally—not a guarantee, but it's a possibility.

Reader, Misha (while she has many strengths) can be (and I don't mean this to be hurtful in any way) <u>foolhardy</u>. She just *decides things*. Without *thinking them through*.

For instance, her plan to get our book published. It would make no sense for Gwen's mom to just *take* our book and *read* it.

BUT, if we give her the book <u>*AND*</u> a cover letter explaining who we are, she'll definitely read it, and we have a much, much higher chance of being famous, published celebrities (82 percent).

Here's a draft cover letter I wrote that we can use:

"Dear Ms. Rossi,

We are classmates of your daughter. Please find attached our own manuscript for your review. We would be appreciative if you could pass it along to your publisher.

Cordially,

[our names here]"

Now, Misha and Ollie: while I agree the basic plot is very solid, I have nonetheless identified several plot holes we will want to address, such as:

- Why does a mirror appear in a middle school?
- Why do they walk through it?
- Are there teachers around who try to stop them? If not, where are they?
- How does the mirror transport them to another world?
- What is Deltovia? What is the climate there like?
- Why were they put on Earth in the first place?
- How do their powers work?
- What is their relationship to the people who were their parents on Earth?
- Will those people miss them when they're in Deltovia?
- Do their parents on Deltovia miss them?

- Why not just teleport them one at a time from their homes?

- Is the mirror some kind of trans-dimensional wormhole?

- Why a mirror, and not some other kind of portal-shaped object?

- Like a door?

- What does everything look like?

- Why weren't they transported through a door?

Fortunately, I have identified possible ways to rescue the story from its biggest plot holes and certain doom, at least for now, which are as follows:

1) All the middle schoolers are originally from Deltovia but were trapped on Earth by an Evil Force.

2) All the middle schoolers are from Deltovia and were put on Earth to *keep them safe* from an Evil Force.

3) All the middle schoolers are on Earth until they have to fight a Battle Royale to the death with each other in Deltovia.

In the last one, the middle schoolers have been kept on Earth, possibly to keep them safe or possibly because of a curse, but they are allowed to cross into Deltovia if they fight a massive battle against each other.

A vote seems like the fairest way for us to decide which of these we want. I will exclude myself from voting since I came up with all three options. Misha, Ollie: Please let me know what you think is best. If you don't like any of them, that is OK, too, and I will try again. Please do not feel like you can't be honest. We can vote anonymously if you'd prefer.

While you are considering the options, I will keep working on my character, Jayana. Jayana has the power to transform anything that exists into anything else that exists. For instance, she can turn a molecule of air into a sword or her enemies into rocks.

I've sketched a couple very quick initial character designs below:

(Preparing to transform anything she wants into anything else she wants)

But returning to the matter at hand, it is essential that we decide on one of these three options, or decide that none of them are good enough, in which case I will start over again. Again, that is fine and you can be honest. We should meet at the Activity Fair this afternoon, in the corner by the end of the bleachers where Misha and I sit during P.E., to pick one option to proceed with.

This may be the most important decision we make in the entire book, so we should be sure to pick very carefully and after much prolonged thought.

September 9th

Great suggestions, June!!! I vote for all of them!!! Misha, you can throw the book like a Frisbee to me any time—I love Frisbee!!

I'll be a little busy at the fair because I'm splitting my time between three tables. I'll swing by, though!! Leave some blank spaces for me!!

Did you two hear that they're not doing snacks after the fair?

J.T. Fleet (bleh) said it was because the school can't afford anything nice, and then he was like, "Isn't it weird that houses around here are so nice but the school isn't?"

And then Tony C. woke up long enough to tell J.T. he was a jerk who didn't know anything, and then J.T. went into his whole speech about his mom and the PTO, and I started tuning him out.

We can def afford some things, though!! There's that big renovation project that's happening this year!! Plus, Coach Kim told me the field trip this year is an overnight trip to the city for the science museum!

Maybe we can room together if I'm not with the soccer, tennis, or lacrosse club. See you at the Activity Fair!

CHRONICLES OF DELTOVIA: CHAPTER 1

"Ugh, the Activity Fair . . . " thought Melodia as she walked into the crowded room. It was loud and busy, which was very different from her lonely life at home, which was lonely because she was an orphan who lived alone.

Jayana looked around the gym and quickly constructed a mental map. It looked like this:

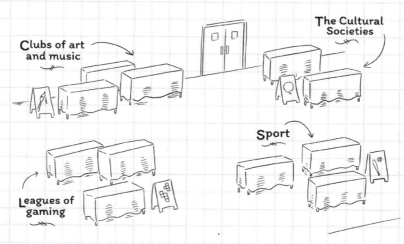

She observed that the only people around were students. This was because all the teachers were at a meeting happening at the exact same time as the Fair on the other side of the school. She gazed around the gym cautiously.

Ollie was _____ there too _____.

As always, Melodia saw how different she was from everyone else. She saw how nobody else had pale purple eyes like her and how they all looked so happy and carefree. She smirked to hide her feelings and blend in . . . when suddenly a cracking sound burst through the room!

CHRONICLES OF DELTOVIA: CHAPTER 2

As the fog cleared, everyone saw that a portal had appeared in the middle of the room. The portal was a mirror because a mirror reflects a person's true self.

Jayana thought it could have been a door, but nonetheless noted that it had appeared approximately here:

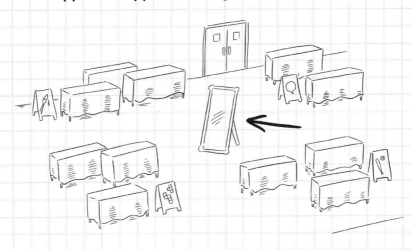

_____ Everyone gasped!!! _____.

Melodia felt like the mirror was calling to her and she couldn't stop her feet from walking toward it—and neither could anyone around her.

The mirror had a gravitational pull, Jayana realized. Everyone was being drawn toward it by forces outside their control, specifically gravity.

One by one, all the students walked through the mirror and disappeared. Melodia sensed something big was going to happen and put on a brave face even though she knew another devastating tragedy in her life could break her to the core.

"_____Same tbh_____," said Ollie.

They were sucked into the mirror, and lights and colors swooshed around them. Everyone was screaming and screaming.

"Ah," Jayana noted. "This is a trans-dimensional wormhole."

They landed in a field, and it was a bright day outside, and almost immediately Melodia realized she had been transformed. Now she had psychic lightning powers and a single demon bat wing on her back.

She also felt that there was something book-shaped in her pocket, but she didn't look at that yet.

Jayana felt different right away. She sensed she could transform anything she wanted into anything else she wanted. She turned a single blade of grass into a staff. Then she turned the staff into a staff that was also a force-field generator.

Ollie was _____ an elf _____.

A voice from above got their attention. They looked and in front of them was a mysterious being with long white hair and pointy ears. "Welcome to Deltovia," he said.

CHRONICLES OF DELTOVIA: CHAPTER 3

The stranger stared at the students. He looked like this:

From a different angle, he looked like this:

Everyone was quiet as he began to speak.

"You were put on Earth to keep you safe from a great evil," he said.

<u>Everyone gasped!!!</u>

"You didn't remember this world because you were cursed as you left Deltovia."

<u>   Everyone gasped!!!   </u>.

"And now you are back home, at long last."

<u>   Everyone sighed   </u>.

"To fight a Battle Royale to the death."

<u>   Everyone gasped!!!   </u>.

"Why?" Melodia asked. She sounded cool and casual on the outside, but on the inside she was full of suffering at the thought of having even more pain in her life.

The being's eyes filled with sorrow and a gentle breeze began to blow behind him. He looked out sadly at the group gathered before him as he explained.

Melodia didn't know what to do or say, but before she could do or say anything, a beam of psychic energy flew right past her head.

The Battle Royale had begun, Jayana observed.

"<u>   Dang   </u>," thought Ollie.

September 16th

June, Ollie—I've been reading the first chapters of our book over and over again, and all I can say is

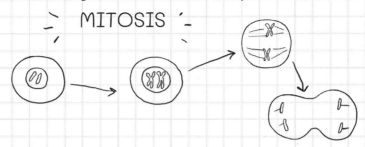

Sorry, Dr. Pendleton just stood behind me so I had to pretend to be taking notes. She's almost as bad as Mrs. Hargrove when it comes to getting on my case. What I was trying to say was

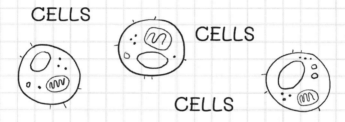

that our story is already shaping up to be the dark, cool masterpiece I knew we were capable of. It's two thousand times better than *The Candelabra* was at this point. When the world reads it, they're going to be deeply, emotionally moved, and then they're going to invite us to be interviewed for TV.

Yes, I suppose we *do* see the world differently from everyone else

(AUDIENCE OOHS)

That school trip sounds interesting, Ollie. Maybe we can get ideas for the book while we're there? Something like:

Ugh, J.T. Fleet is just the worst. His mom has had it out for me ever since the thing with Greg Janssen and Lana M. last year. I saw her and Mrs. Hargrove talking this morning, which makes perfect sense. They're a pair made for each other. I couldn't hear what they were saying to each other, but I suspect it was something like this:

PROBABLY WHAT THEY WERE SAYING

Reader, Mrs. Hargove is the oldest teacher on staff at this school, and she's SUPER strict. She's got this thick Southern accent, which she uses to make it extra memorable and awful when she calls your homework "passable" in front of the rest of the class. I heard a few years ago she made Candace Mitchell's older brother cry for writing a bad poem. She never raises her voice, but that just means she sounds the same whether she's handing you a worksheet or giving you detention for a century.

I knew to watch out for her ahead of time, but I was still surprised when she introduced herself to the class this year like this:

She's the opposite of Mr. Nolan, who's our cool Geography teacher. He puts memes into all his lectures, which appeals to my advanced sense of humor, and he gives everyone in the class nicknames.

Capital of
Louisiana,
Mish-Mash?

Coach Kim is also a cool teacher, though her voice sounds kind of growly all the time.

LAPS

AND SPEAKING OF COOL THINGS: I almost forgot the most important thing that happened today! I was running a little late to school and was almost to the door when *who* should I run into but *Gwen and her mom.*

Our interaction went down a little something like this:

The videos Gwen's mom makes are mostly about lifestyle and wellness, so I wasn't sure how much convincing we'd need to do to get her to read our fantasy epic. But based on today, it seems like she's already taken a *pretty serious* liking to me.

Anyway, we're definitely going to be famous now, and nothing's going to stand in our way, because

SOMETHING SOMETHING

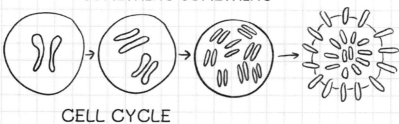

CELL CYCLE

September 17th

Misha, I have to admit that I was unsure how we were going to do it when we first started writing. I expected we would make it through a paragraph, or maybe a sentence, before the burdens of writing a story became too much for us. But looking at our first chapters now, I find myself . . . pleasantly surprised.

This doesn't mean we can relax! We still need to plot out the next arc of the story, and we also need to go back to the parts we left unfinished in "Chapter 3," but I'll admit that the parts we left to be decided later were indeed barely noticeable.

Now, I think we should discuss the overnight trip more. I have a couple questions. Is there a curfew? What are you allowed to bring? Is it just going to be students in the rooms or chaperones? Ollie, if you know something we don't, please let us know as soon as possible.

Mrs. Fleet is definitely going to be a chaperone, and all the teachers are going to be there, too, including Coach Kim!!

How fancy is it?

Does everyone get a room to themselves? Do we get to choose who we room with? How will we get food?

Is it SUPER fancy?

What about transport? Ollie, will you room with us or with your lacrosse friends? I respect your choice either way, but I would like you to know that I deeply treasure and value our friendship.

Let's talk at lunch!!!

CHRONICLES OF DELTOVIA: CHAPTER 4

Melodia didn't know where she was when she woke up and she looked around in confusion. She was in a large room with three fancy beds with curtains and a fountain in the middle. It was super fancy.

The last thing she remembered was the battle—and then she sat upright. Was she even on Earth anymore?

"You're not on Earth anymore," said Jayana, who was already awake and reading a large book. "We're in the magical land of Deltovia, and our room looks like this."

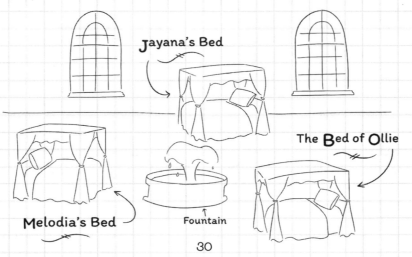

Jayana's Bed

The Bed of Ollie

Melodia's Bed

↑ Fountain

Melodia didn't know what that meant, but before she could ask, she was distracted by a terrible ache in her wing, and she looked and saw she was injured from the terrible battle.

"Yes," Jayana explained. "We were in a terrible battle. But the battle was merely a ruse, an Ancient Ritual to have us form tighter bonds with our allies and learn about our powers. Many people still died, however. Now we are in the dorms of healing, recovering so we can prepare to be trained to fight the Vile One."

"The Vile One . . ." thought Melodia as a strange shiver went down her back.

"_____OK_____," said Ollie, who _____was there_____.

Suddenly, an ear-splitting crack erupted in the room!

CHRONICLES OF DELTOVIA: CHAPTER 5

It was a knight knocking on the door.

I see you're awake! Welcome, young royals. You have survived the Battle Royale

Now, you must rest up, so that you are in top shape to defeat the Vile One

Melodia thought back on the battle. It had been her, Ollie, and Jayana versus everyone else from their school. This was the way of the world. You and your friends versus everyone else. She had shed a single tear about how dark and gritty it all was, and then she'd used her psychic lightning to blast the chess club away.

Jayana had turned several air molecules into nets and used them to trap her opponents without having to physically fight them.

You've fallen for my trap.

Enemies within

Ollie _____ used elf powers _____.

"Tomorrow your training begins," said the knight and left. Melodia fell back into the sheets she was lying on. Even though she had a hurt wing and now had a new scar going across her eye so that she looked like this,

she was still excited for the training.

Jayana observed that she was also excited.

"_____Dang_____," thought Ollie who,
_____was happy_____.

Yet none of them noticed the dark, sinister shadow that quietly slipped into the room through the open window . . . . .

CHRONICLES OF DELTOVIA: CHAPTER 6

"WAIT, I forgot one important thing," said Melodia. She reached into her pocket and pulled out the book-shaped thing she had felt in her pocket when they first arrived in Deltovia. It was a book. But not just any book.

"That's *The Tome of Destiny*," noted Jayana. "A legend in Deltovia says that it holds the power to defeat the Vile One."

"It looks like it chose us as its rightful owners," said Melodia. "We should keep it a secret until we're ready to use it."

Jayana agreed. "I vote we make all decisions about it after serious debate and discussion," she said.

"____K, sounds good_____," said Ollie.

They drifted off to sleep again, feeling completely peaceful.

Yet none of them noticed the SECOND dark, sinister shadow that quietly slipped into the room through a different window than the last one . . . . . .

September 28th

I told my mom about the field trip to see if she knew anything about it, and she didn't seem nearly half as interested in the fact that I, her only daughter, was going to sleep over in a new city, alone, as she should have been.

Reader, this is a total My Mom move. She acts way too casual about some things, and then way too serious about others.

Mom, I'm going to be writing a dark fantasy epic that will make me extremely rich and famous

Sounds great, honey

Mom, I'm going out with my cool, interesting backpack that has at most one or two holes

PLEASE take the one I bought you last year...PLEASE take the one that doesn't look like a bear chewed on it

↑
OVERDRAMATIC

It's not like I need her to look out for me, but I'd at least like to see a little concern for my life and well-being.

Luckily, Mr. Nolan had some more details for us in geography the next day.

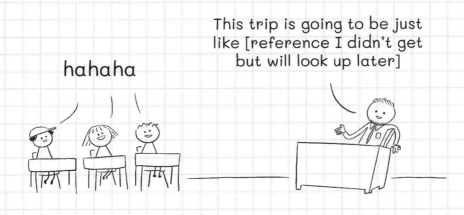

Then I had to do group work with Candace, Mike, and Tony C., which went about like you'd expect.

HALF THIS:

HALF THIS:

I am firmly committed to not letting anyone see our book until we're done with it. Having my mom show *The Candelabra* to her friends like it was the cutest thing ever was extremely disruptive to my creative process. While Deltovia is obviously much more sophisticated and interesting than *The Candelabra* was, I just don't want to risk it.

So I spent a lot of class strategically hunching to make sure Mike couldn't see anything.

But I was able to do some people-watching from my hunched position, which will be helpful for our story. We can use it as inspiration for good side characters. Through the transformative power of fiction, we'll be able to make them far more deep, interesting, and complex than they are in real life.

It's what makes art ART

I'm thinking Candace's power in Deltovia could be that she talks to bugs. And Mike could hover, like, a couple inches off the ground.

Then they could undergo major character development in the story as part of their emotional journey.

AT FIRST:

She only has one wing!
She could NEVER defeat The Vile One

Come along, bugs

BUT BY THE END:

She did it...she defeated The Vile One...

I was so wrong, bugs. I was so very wrong

Tony C.'s power in Deltovia would be . . . hard to say. He's asleep 85 percent of the time. It's hard to craft a character when you've got that little to work with.

I don't believe any of the rumors about *why* he's so sleepy:

But I guess I am curious. Let's put him down as a wind mage for now.

Gwen is also in Geography with me. I'm thinking we get her on our side through some good, old-fashioned schmoozing, and then she can put in a good word with her mom for us.

Here are the things I already knew about Gwen:
- One of Candace's friends
- Quiet

Here are things I've learned about Gwen from my people-watching today:
- Owns a blue pencil case

So, not a full picture yet, but a solid start. To be honest, she kind of reminds me of someone, even though I can't figure out who. But if I do, that will be more stuff to add to my "List of Things I Know about Gwen" list.

Anyway, we didn't get the group project done, but it's not like Mr. Nolan cares about things like that.

Then in English, Mrs. Hargrove called on me to summarize chapter five and wouldn't even let me explain that I *was going* to read chapter five, just as soon as I finished my in-depth analysis chapters of one through four, which I also was going to start reading soon.

Well, as you know from your in-depth reading of the classroom rules, Miss Misha, that means you get a zero for today

MISUNDERSTOOD

Reader, my grades in elementary school were very good. The fact that my grades in middle school are only OK has nothing to do with my smartness and everything to do with the fact that, as a creative genius, I sometimes have other things on my mind. *Some* people (teachers, my mom, June— no offense June) don't fully appreciate this.

I was so annoyed afterward that I went back into the class-room fifteen minutes after class ended. Sure, this was mostly because I had noticed that my calculator wasn't in my back-pack anymore, which usually means it's fallen through one of the holes, but it was also because I wanted Mrs. Hargrove to see how wounded I still was by her hurtful words.

I put on my most authentic "I have been wounded" face and pushed the door open. When I walked in, though, she was on her *phone*.

This is the lady who said she'd write us up if she so much as heard a single notification ding, which is hard for me per-sonally since my mom always wants me to keep the ringer on to make sure I hear her calls.

Mrs. Hargrove barely noticed me—she just looked up and waved me in, then looked back down again. I think it was because she was totally absorbed in whatever she was talk-ing about on the phone.

I didn't hear anything the other person was saying to her, but right before I snuck back out with my calculator, she said, "Well, they better not think they can get that past *me*."

Her voice was the same as it always is, super quiet and low. But trust me (June, Ollie, adoring future fan): she sounded *deadly serious*.

September 29th

Misha, you can't simply make Candace and Mike characters in our story like that. They need backstories, motivations, and magical power names. I've started working on it below with some quick sketches, but certainly there's refining to be done.

CANDACE: Proposed name: Centipedia
POWER: Insectile telepathy, achieved through molecular vibrations.
MOTIVATION: Entire village killed by poisonous gas from another student with pesticide power (?).

If only I could fly...but I cannot

MIKE: Proposed name: Graviton
POWER: Microscale gravity fluctuations.
MOTIVATION: Wants to fly but it is physically impossible for him.

Candace is in homeroom with me, so I'll observe her as well for character inspiration. I already know her fairly well from elementary school, but we can add, based on today, that she owns a purple pencil case.

Your encounter with Mrs. Hargrove sounds harrowing. I wonder what she was so upset about. You're sure she wasn't talking to you, right? You weren't trying to get past her holding something she didn't want you to take?

September 30th

Hey girls!! Great job on the new characters!! Can't wait to add them to the story!! Keep leaving spaces for me to fill in!!

Oh, and by the way. . . . .

Letter to parents:

We are delighted to announce our upcoming field trip to the Science Museum. Below you will find key information about the trip for your planning purposes. A list of items your student will need to bring is provided at the end of this letter.

What are the rules of this trip?

All students will be expected to follow school guidelines, as well as to adhere to the rules of the museum. Appropriate dress is expected. Students will be supervised at all times and will not be allowed out of the chaperoned zones.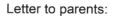

CHRONICLES OF DELTOVIA: CHAPTER 7

"It all makes sense now," Melodia thought. "The reason why I was so different from other people my age . . . it's because I wasn't from Earth and because I also have psychic lightning powers, and now I finally belong. But I'm also still different from everyone because I only have one wing and this scar."

Deltovia, by the way, has a climate very similar to Earth, with some minor exceptions. There are anti-gravity trees, which are empty spaces shaped like trees but full of things that float in space in the shape of a tree because there is no gravity there. The oceans are also pink for microplankton reasons.

Melodia looked around the room with the fountain and her friends.

It was time for their very first day of training . . .

It was time for them to face the other kids from their school, who had tried to kill them just the day before at the Battle Royale . . .

It was time . . . for them to go downstairs . . . to meet . . . their destiny . . .

<u>They did it</u>.

The main courtyard of the Deltovian Royal Academy is between four spikes with a raised platform in the middle. The four spikes represented the four ideals of good citizens of Deltovia: Hard Work, Diligence, Scrupulousness, and Trying Hard. The Academy is in Central Deltovia, not far from the Rose Sea. Jayana knew all of this because she had read all the books about Deltovia while recovering.

A person in purple robes stood on top of the platform, looking stern and holding a magical microphone.

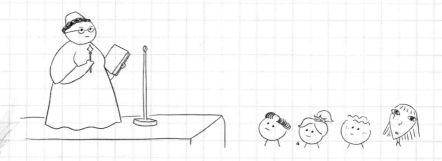

Everyone gathered around. Melodia bumped into a wind mage along the way and asked him who the person in purple robes was.

That's the Witch of Language

YAAAWN

Jayana knew from her studies that wind mages made the wind happen by creating temperature changes in the air. Of course, because Jayana could turn anything she wanted into anything else she wanted, she could also turn hot air into cool air to create wind.

"Young royals," said the Witch of Language all at once in a stern voice. "You must learn to control your powers here at our academy. Only if you do that will you be able to survive when we go to the Supreme Magical Circle in approximately nine weeks to awaken your full powers."

Everyone gasped!!!

Jayana didn't remember there being a Supreme Magical Circle in Deltovia. As she had already learned everything about the world through intense study in her few days in Deltovia, she looked to

Melodia to explain why there was suddenly a Supreme Magical Circle in Deltovia.

"Yes," said the Witch of Language. "The Supreme Magical Circle is a place in Deltovia that definitely exists. It is where you get your powers leveled up."

"Melodia," said Jayana. "We need to have a conversation about how powers work in Deltovia so you can understand what I've been learning from all of my studies. For starters, there's no such thing as levels."

Ollie was _____excited to level up_____.

"Of course, when we are at the Supreme Magical Circle, you will need to stay within my sight at all times for your safety. No leaving that zone," said the Witch of Language.

She looked out seriously at all the students.

"Don't even think you'll be able to get past me," she said.

October 6th

Yesterday, I was sitting outside on my porch, working on character design, when a gust of wind blew a huge number of leaves in front of me in a swirling pattern. At first, I thought it was the universe sending me a sign, so I stopped what I was doing and waited to see what wisdom the wind was going to reveal.

Universe...
I'm ready

Then I looked to my left and saw they were actually just getting blown off of the leaf pile in our neighbor's yard. It was a false alarm destiny. Destiny can be very sneaky like that.

We figured out that Mrs. Hargrove must have been talking about school chaperone zones when she said that whole "nobody could get past her" thing. That's just like her.

Nobody is getting out of class until somebody tells me what Tolkien means here

Nobody is leaving this room until I get an example of a preposition

With all the focus on our novel writing, I totally lost track of time! I didn't realize we're already in October, which means

Halloween is right around the corner. Reader, the three of us have a lot of experience with Halloween over the years.

Back when we were younger, we'd wear themed costumes that matched as a group:

This year, we'll probably dress in ways that highlight our individual styles. Like, I can be a dark celestial being or something.

Then, as is tradition, we'll all go trick-or-treating while June's dad follows us from thirty feet away to make sure we don't get kidnapped.

Speaking of dads, mine called us last night from McMurdo. The reception was really bad, but he said all the normal lovey-dovey stuff to me and my mom.

Having a dad in Antarctica sounds cool, but it's actually super boring. All you get is a bunch of pictures of snow.

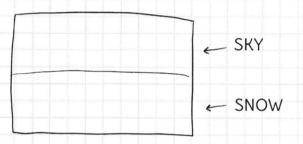

← SKY

← SNOW

And Reader, before you ask, I've checked:

Meanwhile, Gwen's mom gets to be extremely popular and famous on the internet. It makes me so jealous that Gwen gets to live with the person who posted this:

♡ STANDING UP FOR YOURSELF:
My Experiences
1.2M views

And I'm related to the person who posted this:

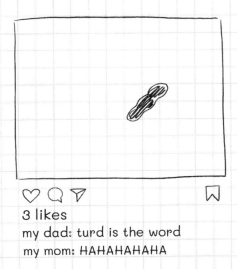

3 likes
my dad: turd is the word
my mom: HAHAHAHAHA

Last night I tried to show my mom some of Gwen's mom's videos last night, and she was nowhere near as impressed as she should have been.

But the research I did will definitely help us win her over to our side. I can even sneak some lines from her videos into Melodia's dialogue. A little flattery like that won't hurt the story but CAN help us win her over to our side. Something like:

Oh, and I had a thought: let's use the creepy energies of this month to write a SCARY chapter. Something really suspenseful and exciting. If there's anybody who understands suspense, it's . . . .

. . . .
. . . .
. . . . us.

October 9th

Dear Misha,

Let's vote on having a creepy chapter. I personally think our priority should be addressing the open plot holes, but if the rest of the group wants to add a creepy chapter, we can add a creepy chapter. I have no problems with a creepy chapter. We can vote on it.

Your friend,
June

Dear Reader,

That is, assuming Misha doesn't get expelled first. Yesterday, at lunch, Greg Janssen's friend Kyle threw a piece of pineapple from one table over which landed on my lunch tray.

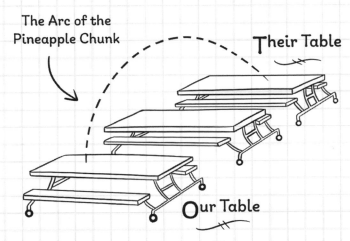

The Arc of the Pineapple Chunk

Their Table

Our Table

I don't think he was aiming at us, and I was prepared to pick it off my tray and not eat the beans it had landed in. Before I could stop her, Misha plucked the pineapple chunk off my plate and threw it back at Kyle, hitting him in the shirt.

Immediately, I began looking around to see if a teacher had seen what she had done and was coming over to take disciplinary action against her. Meanwhile, Misha was totally unconcerned:

It's fine.

It's not like I would have thrown it back if it had landed on some random person's plate

Reader, I know there's a chance I may seem like I worry too much. I know there's a possibility I seem like a (not to use too strong a term) worrywart. Please trust me when I say that there are reasons why I act this way around Misha. And by reasons, I mean "The Incident."

In the end, Misha got away with throwing the pineapple back unnoticed, except by Kyle's friends, who all went "ohhh" when she got him in the shirt.

Yours,
June

October 9th

Great idea on a scary chapter!! Great idea also to fix plot holes!! I vote for both!

CHRONICLES OF DELTOVIA: CHAPTER 8

The Royal Academy had seemed like a nice normal school when Melodia had arrived there, but the longer she spent there, the more she noticed that it was actually very creepy. There were places with lots of fog, for example. And spiders.

But the spookiest thing of all . . . was *The Veil.*

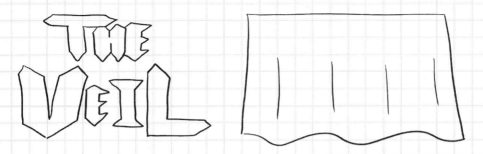

Jayana, separately, had learned that the parents that had raised them on Earth were astral projections of their real parents on Deltovia. So nobody was left behind on Earth missing them, and their Deltovian parents had not missed them while they were gone, either.

This was true for most people, but Melodia was an orphan, so she didn't have Earth parents or Deltovian parents, and nobody could explain why she only had one wing. "Maybe. . ." she thought as she looked out at The Veil. "Maybe this holds the answers."

Jayana was pretty sure it didn't. But she considered it a good possibility.

The Veil was a large, drapey sheet in the middle of the Academy. Behind it was pure darkness. It flapped eerily in the wind . . . and no one knew from whence it came . . .

October 15th

Some behind-the-scenes tidbits for you, Reader. The Veil was inspired by a *real thing* at our school. Basically, there were a bunch of classes that were moved to trailers in the parking lot at the beginning of the year, but they only recently blocked off the part of the school where the construction's going to start. As of last week, there's now a big plastic sheet taped up at the school, cutting off an entire hallway on the second floor.

It's a little annoying because the stairs it connects to were convenient to take, but overall, I think it's a good addition, atmospherically.

A weird thing already happened with it, by the way! I was in-between classes when I happened to walk by. Mrs. Hargrove was next to the big plastic sheet, and she was just staring at it. It's not too far from her classroom, so it wasn't that weird for her to be there, but it was still . . . strange. There's just not much to see.

Maybe she was actually just looking at the PTO's Teacher Appreciation Week decorations. To be fair, they WERE pretty crappy this year.

ENHANCE:

Thanks, teachers

Anyway, all signs are pointing to the undeniable fact that we're going to have our best, creepiest Halloween yet, and nothing can get in the way of that.

October 28th

BAD NEWS GANG: I can't make trick-or-treating this year. :(Lacrosse team is making a recruitment video where we all dance like zombies. Coach Kim says this will be good team bonding. Have fun without me!! Miss you two!!

October 31st

Dear Reader,

This is June. Our Halloween plans have been somewhat disrupted by the weather, so I'm going to take this chance to insert some quick material into our novel while Misha tries to summon a ghost in the bathroom with the lights out.

CHRONICLES OF DELTOVIA: CHAPTER 9

That night, Jayana took out an encyclopedia on the lore of Deltovia and began to read.

Deltovia, she learned, existed in another dimension from Earth. In this dimension, humans can interact with and change the physical laws of nature. In doing this, they achieve "powers." While there is no such thing as "levels" for these powers, gaining more control over your powers is casually referred to as "leveling up."

Happy with this new knowledge, Jayana put the encyclopedia down and went to bed.

CHRONICLES OF DELTOVIA: CHAPTER 10

Jayana didn't notice this because she went to sleep, but in the dark of their pitch-black room there was, for a second, a ghostly face that appeared in the window and looked at them all sleeping. It didn't blink and it hovered in the air. Again, they didn't notice it, but it was very creepy.

October 31st

OK, so our trick-or-treating plans didn't work out exactly the way we wanted. First, Ollie had sports and couldn't make it; then it started pouring outside; then my attempt to summon Bloody Mary just ended up with me accidentally scaring June's sister when she went to take out her contacts.

Bloody Mary, Bloody Mary, Bloody—

AHHH

AHHHH

AHHH

(LIGHTS ARE OFF)

But June's dad is still checking up on us, so that part's the same.

EVERY FIFTEEN MINUTES

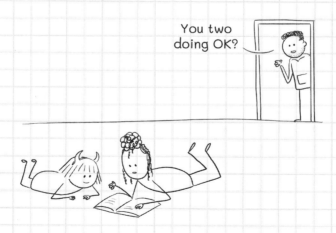

You two doing OK?

Now June and I are on the floor in her room, doing some character design.

We need some obnoxious characters for the audience to hate, so I propose these:

Name: Fleeth
Power: Ability to walk through walls, which he uses to be a big creep.

Name: Grog Jonsson
Power: Really strong, mean, and stupid, but has a lot of friends for some reason.

There's this other character I want to introduce named Gwelle. She starts out as one of the popular girls, but then she meets our heroes and realizes how great they are and decides to help them instead.

And since June's looking over my shoulder insisting that I do this, here's her full character profile:

Power name: ~~shining bright~~ **Luminosopher**

Explanation of power: She can shine bright **with the power of photoluminescence.**

Motivation: To actually meet some interesting people, for once, who understand life in a deep way.

November 2nd

I don't understand lacrosse, but Reader: Ollie's video came out pretty good. I was watching it last night when my mom looked over my shoulder and asked me why I hadn't gone to one of Ollie's games in a while.

This seemed vaguely like an accusation. I tried to explain that just because we're very close doesn't mean we don't each have our own independent interests that make us interesting in our own ways.

Mine is contemplating the mysteries of the human condition; June's is learning everything about everything, and Ollie's is the whole sports thing

And contemplating the mysteries of the human condition takes up a LOT of my energy

Ollie, you know we support you even without coming to your games, right? We don't *need* to go to every game just to show you we care about you!

But June and I decided to go to a game anyway because we're very supportive, and my mom said she would pick us up and get us all ice cream after.

Watching it was a little more interesting than I expected. Plus, I got to see June have her thinking face on the whole time.

Also Mr. Nolan was there, too, and said hi.

Mish-Mash and Junebug!

Didn't take you two for sports enthusiasts

We're here to cheer on our friend. She's kind of the best player

Which position does she play?

Uhhhh

It was cool to see Ollie on the field. She was super fast and super strong. She was like . . . a shining star.

It reminded me of the games we used to play when we were little. When we were really young, we used to play regular old tag, and Ollie would always win.

PLAYING TAG

Then we met June, and our games became more sophisticated.

PRETENDING TO BE HORSES

Fastest horse

These days, we make up characters and stories, so there's not really "winning" anymore. It's all about working together to make the best story. There's not really a "star" or anything like that.

After the game finished, we walked with Mr. Nolan down to where Coach Kim and the team were.

Therese, hey!

Matthew.

You did very well, Ollie

That's right: we're getting ICE CREAM with the STAR

Getting ice cream was strange. It was like being back in the third grade.

We used to be so innocent. I even put a whole scene in *The Candelabra* about a group of friends going to get ice cream that was based on us.

Our new characters would never say anything like that.
Instead we're more like:

Before, when I'd hear the songs they play in the ice cream
parlor, I'd be like:

EXTREMELY SIMPLISTIC

Now I'm like:

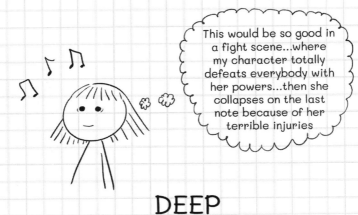

This would be so good in a fight scene...where my character totally defeats everybody with her powers...then she collapses on the last note because of her terrible injuries

DEEP

As I sat there, ideas started to drip into my head. Ideas for scenes where Melodia . . . could totally shine . . .

November 8th

Misha, I was only trying to understand the rules. I am now much more prepared to play lacrosse, in the event that you and I ever play lacrosse in gym instead of sitting in the corner like normal.

On the topic of fight scenes, I should provide a little more information on how Jayana fights. As you know, she can turn anything she wants into anything else she wants. She could win any fight by just turning her enemies into leaves. Her preferred strategy, however, is to win with cleverness, not force. She will often subdue opponents with tricks that they don't see coming. Here's what a typical fight looks like for Jayana:

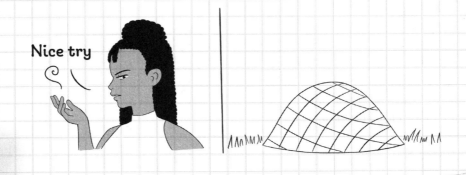

Nice try

I do think it will be good for our school to be renovated. Our sports field is up on a hill, and from the bleachers, I could see the school building and all the trailers they've set up in the parking lot for classes during construction.

It's tedious to have to take classes in trailers, but the sacrifice is worth it to make the school a better, safer place. It's something the school as a whole needs to care about more. As we know, there are basic safety measures, like locking the gate that keeps people away from the roof access ladder, that were put into place only recently.

Regards,
June

November 9th

Thanks, you two!! Southbrook Middle almost gave us a run for our money. Coach Kim says they've got four people who might make All-County.

Glad we pulled it off AND I'm glad you got to see the team!! We should all hang out together sometime. I think you'd get along with Autumn and Yvonne. They're great, and I bet they'd have a lot of ideas for our story!!

Ahhh that sounds fun and COULD work, but I'm kind of thinking this is really more of a "the three of us" thing. Right, June? I'm passing this to June right now for her thoughts.

I agree with Misha. We are a great team, the three of us. Passing this back to Misha to make sure she agrees.

Thanks, June. I do agree. Plus, we don't want to let anyone read it until it's done. Also, remember when we made the JOM Society out of the first initials of all our names in second grade? That was great. Passing this to June.

It was great. Passing back to Misha.

Anyway, we're proud of you, Ollie, and we can't wait to hear how your next game goes! Unrelatedly, I'm feeling inspired to work on the book right now, and since June is only a few seats away in math class, she can help me with this chapter, too.

CHRONICLES OF DELTOVIA: CHAPTER 11

In training class at the Deltovian Royal Academy, Melodia looked over at Jayana and Ollie, her two best friends, and knew it would always be the three of them.

"Yes," Jayana thought to herself. "It will always be us three." They had been together through thick and thin.

They had been right next to each other when they came to Deltovia, and they were going to stick that way as a small but mighty team of three, for all time.

There was no one amongst the assembled crowds Jayana would want to be as close to as she was with Melodia and Ollie. She was confident that she'd never want to spend any time with anyone but those two.

Melodia agreed completely. Except maybe they could spend time with Gwelle as part of the plan to befriend Gwelle.

Jayana didn't know Melodia was trying to get Gwelle as a friend. She thought the plan was to get Gwelle's help, acquaintance-style.

Melodia agreed it would be acquaintance-style help. They would spend time with her like acquaintances do. And since Gwelle's mom was a famous mage in Deltovia who was renowned throughout the lands, if they got to know Gwelle, as acquaintances, they could use her to help them defeat the Vile One.

Jayana reminded Melodia of the last time she tried to befriend someone new and how well that had worked out. "Cough," said Jayana. "Remember *The Incident?* Cough, cough."

Melodia respected Jayana's opinions but thought she was maybe worrying way too much.

Jayana respected Melodia's opinions but thought she was perhaps not being cautious enough.

Melodia turned to Ollie to get her thoughts on what she thought they should do.

Ollie said,

" _____ Great ideas!!!!! _____

_____ I vote for all of them!!! _____."

November 15th

For research the other day—JUST RESEARCH—I decided to track down Gwen's mom's book. It's called *Genevieve Unadorned*.

They didn't have a copy at the school library, so I had to go to the county library, where they had, like, four.

It's basically full of pictures of Gwen's mom, nice things, and these short motivational essays on how to be the person you want to be.

Gwen's in it, too, a bunch of times.

From Chapter 4, "Home and Hearth"

I wasn't sure how interested I'd be in it since it doesn't really have a plot or characters, but I did end up enjoying myself. I get why Gwen's mom is so popular online. There's lots of advice on stuff that does actually matter, now that I think of it. Like believing in yourself and having good morning routines.

One thing that stuck with me was how much Gwen was smiling in the pictures. She really doesn't do that a lot in school, I guess. It helped me add more to my "List of Things I Know about Gwen" list.

List of Things I Know about Gwen:
  - Likes candles
  - Likes waffles with berries

I walked to school deep in thought about ways I could add morning routines to the plot of our book.

On my way to first period (slightly late, not a big deal), I overheard a conversation between Dr. Pendleton and Mr. Tranh, the custodian, who were in the teacher's lounge with the door open.

Gang, I'm not so sure Mrs. Hargrove was talking about the trip when she was all like, "You can't get past me," before. It's not that I saw her be *deadly serious* again (I didn't), but Dr. Pendelton and Mr. Tranh were definitely talking about her, using her first name (Marcia Hargrove, check the yearbook).

Marcia is really serious about this. You saw her email, right?

She's going to say something at the school board tonight

Her exact words to me were "I won't let them change the school like this"

I did my best to pick up on what Dr. Pendleton was saying, but maybe I did too good of a job, because she noticed me right when I was almost all the way past her.

In after-school detention, I got on my phone to try to look up what school meeting thing she could have been talking about.

Underneath "Public Forum: Proposition 12" and "Public Forum: Honoring the Achievements of the Anderson Scholars" on the county event calendar, I found it: "Public Forum: Lakeview Middle School Renovations."

They're having a meeting about fixing up our school tonight. And I don't think Mrs. Hargrove wants it to happen.

November 15th

Dear Misha,

That seems very strange. Why would she not want the school to be renovated?

Best wishes,
June

Maybe she just hates change? She's been here forever, and maybe she wants the school to look exactly the way it looked when she arrived. Remember the way she was staring at the big plastic sheet?

Dear Misha,

But why?

Best wishes,
June

I might not know right now, but there has to be SOME reason.

Good theories!! Great work, you two!!

November 22nd

Dear Reader,

With the trip to the Science Museum around the corner, all of our teachers are beginning to panic about getting anything done before winter break.

In their defense, I'll admit not everyone is giving it their best effort. In homeroom today, Candace spent most of her time on her phone. I'm not sure how people who do that expect to succeed in life.

My sister, who is a few years older than me, says middle school is way easier than high school. But I believe middle school is just getting harder every year. One challenge is that the books we're assigned to write reports on are *full* of plot holes.

J.T. Fleet likes to complain that the standards at our school aren't as good as the private schools in the area, but I don't see how he can say that when he's barely scraping together a B+ in most of his classes.

Dear Misha and Ollie:

An interesting piece of information went home about the field trip yesterday. Did you see that? Apparently, all the attendees are supposed to bring a sleeping bag with them. Is there some kind of camping component to the trip we weren't told about?

Your friend,
June

November 23rd

I saw that!! I asked Coach Kim, and she just said it's a surprise. Maybe we're going into the woods? We'll see, I guess, haha!!

December 10th

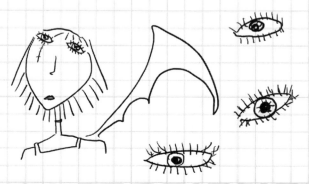

Everyone knows that half the fun of a school trip is the bus ride out there. June and I managed to get seats next to each other, and Ollie's only a couple rows behind us with some people from the lacrosse team. They're playing *Jurassic Park* on the tiny screens at the front, which makes no sense since everybody's got their phones on them. The guy in front of me is just watching *Jurassic Park* on YouTube, five minutes behind the bus video.

This morning everyone had to wake up super early to load up the buses. And since my mom's shifts can start pretty early, she dropped me off with my bags EVEN EARLIER than I needed to be there. I sat on the curb for like forty-five minutes while everybody else trickled in, so I decided to use the time to do warm-up drawings. Of course, SOME people refused to let me simply be a genius in peace.

Hey Misha, you writing something?

NO

Mike lives down the street from us, and his mom is friends with my mom, so I'm *extra* wary of him passing along information about this notebook. The good news is most of the time, he and the rest of his crew don't notice I exist.

That's true of a lot of people at our school. My friends and I aren't what you'd call "popular," but we're definitely not unpopular, either. I guess you'd say most other people leave us alone. They don't really pay attention to what's right under their noses. Not that I mind, since they're nowhere near as interesting as June, Ollie, and me, but it did mean that I was sitting by myself until June got dropped off.

As I looked out at the other kids standing around, I decided
I needed to start getting their attention more. I decided
to use this trip to get closer to Gwen and her mom, as
acquaintances. Since she's chaperoning the trip, it's a
perfect opportunity to get a lot of uninterrupted time with
her. Here's how it will go down, if all goes according to plan:

Don't you think
floral print
wallpapers are
going to be big
this spring?

Yes, but how...

...did you see
that in one of
my videos?

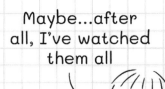
Maybe...after all, I've watched them all

DELIGHTED
↓

HOW IT WILL GO

Now's as good a time as ever to get some story writing done, since I've had these scene ideas kicking around in my head for a while, and I don't have enough data to stream the whole ride. And since June is unavailable.

I am not going to write while carsick, please stop trying to make we write while carsick, Misha

I'll just tackle these next few chapters on my own.

CHRONICLES OF DELTOVIA: CHAPTER 12

The day had come for the class to go to the Supreme Magical Circle to level up. Their guide (the one who had welcomed them to Deltovia and whose name we forgot to mention is Azariel) led the way.

The journey will be long and hard and you will have to do some camping

AZARIEL

The Witch of Language, the head wizard, the knight, and Gwelle's mother (the Mage of Light) came along, too, and were carefully watching the students to make sure none of them left the zone of protection that shielded them from the Vile One's evil forces. But Melodia couldn't help but wonder if somehow the group had already been infiltrated by something evil, and she sensed that something bad would happen on this journey.

Everyone was laughing and having a good time as they hiked toward their destination, and nobody except Melodia felt the aura of doom in the air.

"Relax," yawned the wind mage next to her. "Nothing's going to happen."

"Yeah," sneered Fleeth. "You're totally nervous about nothing like some kind of loser."

"Maybe I'm wrong," Melodia thought to herself. She felt all alone in the world yet again.

Suddenly, a cracking sound ripped through the air!

CHRONICLES OF DELTOVIA: CHAPTER 13

The protective barrier that was protecting the students was crumbling to pieces!! All around them, the glowing shield fell away and turned into dust and shattered. All the teachers started scrambling, but none of them were fast enough to stop the dark tendrils of evil from stabbing at the students. They were the dark tendrils of the Vile One!

One was going to hit Jayana! She was about to die. Then, suddenly, Melodia jumped in front of it heroically and protected her from the blow but got tragically stabbed herself.

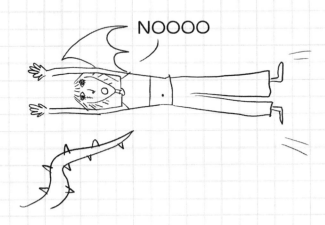

Then another tendril came toward Ollie! Melodia jumped in front of that, too, and declared, "You won't take my friends!" in midair even though she was in pain.

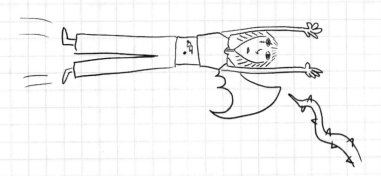

Another tendril was going to hit Gwelle, but Melodia jumped in front of her and protected her as well, and Gwelle looked on in gratitude.

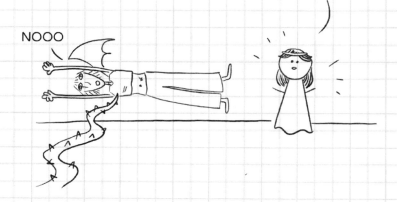

Then Melodia's eyes glowed white and a torrent of lightning came down upon the dark tendrils, forcing them back and defeating the evil for now. The teachers hurried to repair the protective barrier, and eventually they got it up again.

"You saved us," said Azariel, who was blinking tears from his eyes. "You saved us all."

"I was just doing what anyone would do," said Melodia, smirking, and then she passed out from all the stab wounds.

CHRONICLES OF DELTOVIA: CHAPTER 14

Melodia woke up slowly and found herself in a bed in the hospital wing. She sat up and looked around. Her friends were there, and they were so relieved she was OK.

"I'm so relieved you're OK," said Jayana. "Thank you for saving us."

"You are a true hero," agreed Ollie.

Melodia tried to sit up but grimaced with pain.

"Don't try to get up," said Jayana. "You were terribly injured by the tendrils of evil and nearly died protecting the whole class. To fully recover, we think it will take you at least until tomorrow. For now, you should rest and focus on healing up, not the Vile One."

"The Vile One . . . " Melodia said quietly to herself, feeling an ominous shiver in the back of her head.

She felt really tired, but she needed to ask: "Why did the protective shields break up in the first place?"

Her friends looked concerned because that thought hadn't occurred to them. "That thought hadn't occurred to us," Jayana said. "But we will have to keep thinking about it if we want to solve the mystery."

Gwelle came in then and said, "I also want to thank you for saving me, Melodia."

Melodia would have said something in response, but everything faded to white as she passed out again.

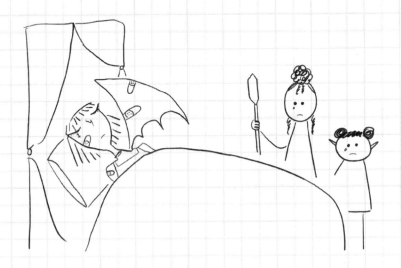

Misha, June, here's why I waved at you to toss the notebook back here: it turns out we're sleeping over IN the museum!!! Like, under dinosaur bones and everything. This was the surprise Coach Kim was talking about!! It's so funny and weird.

I didn't see any blank spaces for me to fill out in the last chapters, but they looked good to me!!

(Still) December 10th

Misha, I know you are looking over my shoulder as I write this and that you're going to want the pen to write something back, but we need to have a conversation about boundaries. From now on, if you want there to be dialogue for a character that isn't your own, you have to leave a blank space for the person to write that in. That way, the person who made the character gets to decide what their character would say. If we don't do this, the book is doomed to fail.

For instance, Jayana would never have said, "That thought hadn't occurred to us." She would definitely have already thought about the need to figure out who among their group is working for the Vile One. Now I need to find a smooth way to go back and fix that in the next chapters, or the book will be ruined.

June.

Dear Misha, again: I'm sorry if I sounded upset in the above. Obviously, I trust your writing and creative vision. But I have to be the one who writes Jayana. You can have the pen back when I'm done.

Your friend,
June

Dear Reader,

We're off the bus now, sitting in an auditorium and watching an hour-long movie about the rules of the museum. I'm very happy to be here, but this is clearly a video aimed at a younger audience than us.

We know it can be scary to spend the night...just down the hall from a shark!

But keep yourself safe with...the BUDDY SYSTEM!

The bus ride out here was long and nauseating. I have no idea why they don't make us all wear seatbelts, but most kids weren't, which was clearly unsafe. Misha, you can have the pen back when I'm finished.

In fact:

CHRONICLES OF DELTOVIA: CHAPTER 15

"That thought hadn't occurred to us," Jayana lied, trying not to upset Melodia since the blood loss had clearly affected her brain. Of course, it had immediately occurred to Jayana that she needed to catch the infiltrator, and she was working around the clock to figure out who was working for the Vile One, using logic and skill.

She was making incredible progress and would probably have everything figured out in a matter of minutes. She got up and decided to go work on that in the other room, leaving Melodia blissfully unconscious behind her.

CHRONICLES OF DELTOVIA: CHAPTER 16

Melodia felt bad for overstepping boundaries and promised she would never make assumptions about what Jayana
would say or do again. She had been wrong to do that. Also,
she was still knocked out—these were just feelings she was
having in her dreams.

CHRONICLES OF DELTOVIA: CHAPTER 17

Jayana paused in the door and looked back on Melodia's sleeping
form. She knew Melodia often did things without thinking. That
was just the way Melodia was. It wouldn't be easy, but Jayana
believed she could find it in herself to forgive her friend. She
turned and headed out of the room.

CHRONICLES OF DELTOVIA: CHAPTER 18

Melodia suddenly sat up in bed!!

"But have you considered that it could be one of the _adults_?"
she asked before Jayana could leave. Then before Jayana
could say anything back, Melodia said, "I trust you will figure it out, Jayana, because you are a great detective, and I
love you. And that's why I had no choice but to jump in front
of the evil tendril to protect you. I know you will figure it out
. . . including if it is maybe one of the adults . . . " And then
her voice drifted away as she passed out once more.

CHRONICLES OF DELTOVIA: CHAPTER 19

Jayana had headphones in, so she didn't actually hear Melodia
say anything, but if she had, all she would have heard was an
idea she'd come up with on her own long ago.

CHRONICLES OF DELTOVIA: CHAPTER 20

Melodia opened her eyes a crack. She could tell Jayana's
headphones were out of battery and that she had heard
her good idea.

CHRONICLES OF DELTOVIA: CHAPTER 21

Melodia did not know this, but Jayana had used her power to turn the batteries that were dead into batteries that worked, so she hadn't heard anything at all.

CHRONICLES OF DELTOVIA: CHAPTER 22

Melodia turned to Ollie to see if she thought the headphones were on or off.

Jayana sighed.

" Both options sound good to me!!! " Ollie said.

December 10th

While I admit this sleeping arrangement is not what I first imagined, it's got a lot going for it. For starters, even though we don't have a room to ourselves, I still get to be near my friends. And the three of us get to be near a woolly mammoth display.

OUR WISE PROTECTOR

Even Mrs. Fleet seems fine with it. She and J.T. were NOT fine with the place we stopped for lunch, which was some kind of buffet where everything looked like mashed potatoes, except the mashed potatoes, which looked like beige slush.

REALLY OBVIOUS NON-WHISPER WHISPER

But she looks perfectly happy over by her Mars Rover. Happy for her, at least.

It's funny how different she acts around Gwen's mom versus the other parents. Around Gwen's mom, she's like:

If you can find the time to sign up for some more PTO volunteering hours, that would be wonderful, Genevieve. But you're already doing so much

But around Candace's dad, she's like:

Sign up for more PTO shifts, Ted.

It's like she knows Gwen's mom is famous but hasn't ever looked at the stuff she's famous *for*. After all:

Why you don't need fake friends

♡ GETTING REAL ABOUT FAKE PEOPLE
400K views

Gwen's mom handles it very politely and all (I found out on the school website that she's doing like two jobs on the PTO), but it has to get boring dealing with people who always want things *from* you, instead of wanting to *give* you something, like an awesome fantasy book they wrote with their friends that you can get published.

Changing into pajamas was a little awkward, but luckily I've developed a technique for changing without ever getting naked.

1. Put on pajamas over regular clothes   2. Shimmy   3. Shimmy   4. Regular clothes removed, pajamas still on

June changed in the bathroom because she does not have my impressive technique.

I'm already feeling inspired by all the weird things at this museum. We didn't have a ton of time to look around this afternoon, but we did get to see the geology section and the ocean section. Of course, we went a little slower than everybody else because June won't move on to the next room until she's read all the little labels for every exhibit.

Mm. Fascinating

I'm pretty sure we got more out of everything than the other kids, though. Greg Janssen and his friends spent the whole time daring each other to touch things past the exhibit signs that said "Don't Touch."

I almost told them to stop, but what's the point. It's not like it's worth sticking my neck out for something like that.

Candace and the other girls from her group mostly hung out around in the space exhibit, talking.

Tony C. tried to take a nap behind one of the interactive tree exhibits and got caught by Mr. Mitchell.

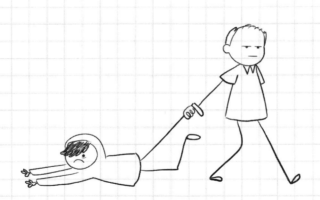

For dinner, they brought us these box lunches with sandwiches and cookies wrapped together in the same plastic wrap, which was OK except it gave the cookies, like, a turkey aftertaste. J.T. Fleet managed to eat his, though he had a "too good for this, am I going to barf" look on his face the whole time.

June and I have talked it over and agreed that even though Jayana totally could figure out who the traitor is because she is smart, we're not going to reveal their identity until close to the end so it happens at the climax of the story.

Speaking of which:

CHRONICLES OF DELTOVIA: CHAPTER 23

Melodia got up from the hospital wing and went down to where everyone was gathered at the Supreme Magical Circle lobby. When she entered, everyone gasped quietly because they knew they owed their lives to her, and a few people could not even hold back their tears of gratitude and started bawling loudly. But because she was so humble, Melodia barely even noticed.

"Melodia, Ollie," Jayana said, walking up to her. "Per our previous conversation, I am very close to uncovering who the villain is. In fact, I have figured it out entirely and am sure I am right. But I am not going to reveal it until later. Why, you ask? Well, certain people seem to think that if I revealed it now, it would mean there would not be enough of a mystery build-up and the reveal would not be satisfying enough, and that I should wait until five, ten, or perhaps one hundred of our classmates have died before sharing this information with the group later on. Yes, no matter how many people are brutally killed, I must keep my keen insights to myself for now, in what some MIGHT call a PLOT HOLE."

"_____K sounds good_____" said Ollie.

Suddenly Gwelle walked by.

"Hi Gwelle," said Melodia, smoothly catching her attention.

"Hi Melodia," said Gwelle. She sounded a little nervous and surprised, probably because she didn't usually hang around people as interesting as Melodia and her friends.

"I was just thinking . . . we should get to know each other better," said Melodia. "We're trying to defeat the Vile One, after all, and we could use your help."

"You really think so?" said Gwelle hopefully.

"Yeah, plus your mom is the Mage of Light, so she could probably be a huge help. We've got the Tome of Destiny, and she sounds like she'd know exactly what we should do with it," said Melodia.

"She IS pretty great," said Gwelle. "She has the power to control light magic, and she is also really famous. Most people we know aren't very deep, though."

"My friends and I are deep," said Melodia.

"That's awesome," said Gwelle, who was really impressed. "I have to tell her about you."

Jayana stepped over and interrupted them, since they had had an appropriate amount of time to talk as acquaintances. "Melodia, it's time to go to the astronomer's tower at the middle of the Supreme Magical Circle, where we shall commune with the stars and deepen our understanding of our powers." She took Melodia and Ollie with her and ascended the stairs of the tower with them both. Gwelle did not come with them.

Ollie was _____ excited to level up _____.

When they reached the top of the astronomer's tower, they found a magnificent library that looked like this:

Ancient lores

Potted plant

Mirror of infinity

The ceiling was covered in stars. It was too beautiful for words to capture. It was super pretty.

There was a wizard there, too, who greeted them:

What's up, kiddos?

Jayana closed her eyes solemnly. "We are here to deepen our connection with the universe so we can better alter the rules of physics as part of our magical powers."

Oh, so you want to level up? Cool, cool. I can do that

Suddenly all the stars on the ceiling lit up and glowed! Then Melodia, Jayana, and Ollie all started glowing, too, and they felt themselves getting stronger.

Specifically, their brains were getting stronger because they were being filled with knowledge of the world. They were understanding the threads of the universe and how they could alter them to make it so they could better control the domains of the world they had magical command over. It was as if all the knowledge in the library was being transferred into their heads.

Suddenly the glowing stopped!

Well, there ya have it. You're all leveled up now

Suddenly Melodia realized how much more powerful she was than she had been mere minutes before.

"Melodia," Jayana said. "Not everything that happens has to happen *suddenly*."

Jayana was happy to have achieved a better understanding of her powers, which was still the ability to turn anything into anything else. All was peaceful and still in the library.

Suddenly the wizard's eyes glowed white!!!!

CHRONICLES OF DELTOVIA: CHAPTER 24

The wizard's eyes were glowing, and he was no longer the happy, laidback guy he had been a couple minutes before. Now he was having a prophecy:

Chosen Ones...I have a prophecy to tell you

The room was darker, and it had a creepy feel to it. Only the stars on the ceiling continued to glow.

He pointed to Jayana first.

"Soon . . . you shall find a Thing . . . that you won't be able to transform into another Thing with your powers."

Jayana strongly disagreed. But she let him continue because he maybe had some smart things to say.

He pointed to Ollie next.

"You will learn to _____ talk to animals _____ !!!!!"

Lastly he pointed to Melodia.

"You, Melodia, will learn . . . . the reason behind the mystery of your missing wing!!"

Melodia gasped. She couldn't wait to learn why she had only one bat wing. Above their heads, the stars on the ceiling swirled and swirled while the wizard's eyes stayed glowing white. Then everything stopped moving, and the wizard's eyes stopped glowing, and he fell to the ground.

"Call for help," Jayana yelled to another student who happened to be near the entrance of the tower. Jayana happened to be trained in first aid as well, so she knew not to move the wizard in case he had a head injury. She was prepared to do CPR if necessary. Luckily, she did not need to because she was able to stabilize the wizard with her skills in just a few minutes.

"I'm healed," said the wizard, sitting up. "But what . . . happened . . . ?"

"You claimed you were telling us 'a prophecy,'" said Jayana.

"Oh, silly me," the wizard said. "That's what I call it when I say random gibberish that nobody should listen to. "

"That explains it," nodded Jayana.

"That nobody should listen to—unless they are the Chosen Ones," he finished. "And if my eyes glowed white and that ceiling did the whole thing, it was definitely a real prophecy that predicts the future."

Then the student came back with the medical aid, and it was time for them to leave, so there was no more talking to the wizard.

None of them noticed the dark shadow sneaking out of the astronomer's tower and following them down the stairs . . . .

(Still) December 10th

We have to be quiet, but I was looking at the dinosaur bones just now while I was waiting to fall asleep, and a thought occurred to me.

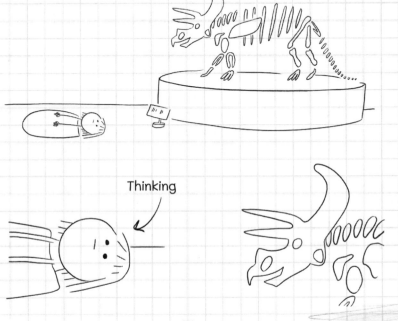

Thinking

Genius idea

Dinosaur bones get discovered when people start digging in new places. What if the reason Mrs. Hargrove doesn't want the school to be renovated is because she doesn't want them to find something when they start tearing the walls down? Something like a SKELETON hidden in the walls of the building? Just a theory I wanted to get down on paper before I forgot.

(Still) December 10th

Dear Misha,

This does seem possible, but unlikely. I give it a 35 percent chance of being true. Still, we shouldn't rule it out. Let's discuss more tomorrow morning.

Best regards,
June

December 11th

Dear Reader,

We have a slight problem. Not with the book, which, despite certain differences of vision between me and Misha, I have no doubt I can rescue.

The problem is that Misha has gotten in trouble on the trip, and I fear she may be expelled from school altogether.

It will be hard for the three of us to stay a group if this happens.

Sure, I'll be able to see Misha during non-school hours, but if she's gone during the school days, and with Ollie having a number of sporting obligations, our hours together will be limited. We can use the notebook to pass thoughts back and forth, but I am not sure how much Misha's reading and writing skills will suffer from her lack of education.

Reader, I . . . I'm worried for her. This is like last year's "The Incident" all over again, and while I agree with Misha that it was primarily Greg Janssen's fault, it's the school administrators who make the decision about who is punished for such things. With that on her record, and now this new infraction, I don't know what's going to happen to her.

Dear Misha,

If you're reading this, they've either let you out, or I've managed to get this notebook into your hands. Maybe we've already spoken. Or maybe this is the first contact you've had from me in weeks. Whichever it is, please, please take care of yourself. Don't tell them anything that could incriminate you. If you do get expelled, I will bring a copy of my homework over to your house so you can do it there. It won't be as good as real feedback from a trained teaching professional, but I will do my best to keep you literate and informed, no matter how much of a struggle it is for both of us.

Your ally,
June

Dear Reader,

Updates: Ollie tells me that she just saw Misha, and that she looks like she's OK and is just sitting over in the cafe area next to the chaperones with a croissant.

I will report back if I learn more.

(Still) December 11th

Nobody panic!! I'm OK, but there's LOTS to discuss.

Yesterday started out pretty normal. June and I made it through 1.5 exhibit halls in the morning, and we were making good progress through the tundra ecosystem after lunch when I saw Gwen standing over by the taxidermied moose.

Mm. Fascinating

Seeing my chance to make an acquaintance, I went over and struck up a casual conversation.

Hey, Gwen!

...hi.

How's it going? Your trip to the museum, I mean

...fine.

And your mom is a chaperone, ri—

Don't we need to head back to the entrance now?

So, not the best, but definitely not the worst. I think she just needs time to warm up to us before she can get how complex, emotionally deep, and interesting we are.

And of course, she was right. At two o'clock they wanted everyone back together in the main lobby so we could walk over to the planetarium (which was in a building attached to the science museum) for a show.

I was pretty determined to end up next to June and Ollie, but that horrible thing happened where you are trying to sit next to your friend but then the row of seats ends, and you have to go sit at the far end of the row behind them and you end up as far as you could possibly be from each other.

Also, Ollie was sitting with her lacrosse friends anyway.

So I ended up next to the wall and Mike.

Luckily, the show started up before we had to have much of a conversation. At first, it was sort of normal. The host started talking about light pollution and the North Star, and I leaned back in my chair.

I can't really describe what happened next. At some point, I stopped listening to the host. In the dark, with the galaxy swooping by overhead, I felt invisible and safe. I felt like a small speck of dust next to something big and eternal and cosmic.

BUT EVEN MORE INCREDIBLY: it was exactly what I'd imagined the astronomer's tower to be like in the last chapter of our story. It was like it had been plucked out of my head and plopped into the real world. It was unreal.

Stuff like that doesn't happen by chance. I knew I was experiencing a real, actual destiny moment.

I had to explore more. I decided to scooch off my chair and hide under the row of seats so I wouldn't have to leave when the lights came on. It was actually pretty easy.

I stayed down there once it ended and stayed put while everyone left. Even though my hiding spot wasn't great, once people started standing up, Mike didn't even notice. It wasn't until I heard the door click and lights dim again and there was silence for a full thirty seconds that I stuck my head out.

27 one hundred...28 one hundred...
29 one hundred...

If being in the planetarium for the main show was cool, being there all by myself was amazing. I ran to the middle and looked up. They had basically a star screensaver on. Just the normal night sky. But I was alone, and I could tell I was going to get an amazing idea for our story.

I could have stayed there forever. It really felt like I was in another world. I was ready for the inspiration to flow in.

And then, suddenly:

Ringtone sounds

And seconds later:

Honestly, of all the places to forget a cellphone...

Sorry, mom

VOICES OF MRS. FLEET AND J.T.

I dived back in between the rows of seats to get out of view. I managed to do it without making too much noise, but as soon as I looked up:

"What are you doing here?" I whispered.

"Hmphwha?" said Tony.

With my skills of deduction, I determined he had been asleep.

"We're about to get caught," I said. "You need to move." He woke up pretty fast after that.

Unfortunately:

ZOOMED OUT VIEW

Ugh, my dad's gonna kill me. There's no hope

Suddenly, against my will, my brain spontaneously decided to remember a line from *The Candelabra*.

There's a zero percent chance of hope!

There's ALWAYS hope!!!

I got the kind of adrenaline you get when you remember something embarrassing. Like when you're in bed at night and you remember an embarrassing thing and it makes you scrunch up into a ball super fast. I needed somewhere for the adrenaline to go. I could hear the door being pushed open.

"Listen," I said. "I'm going to do something that will look really, really cool."

Then I rolled three rows of seats down and stood up.

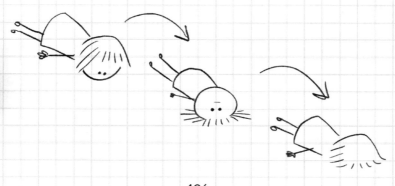

There was a lot of squawking from her then, but all it amounted to was her bringing up the thing with Greg Janssen and Lana M. a few times (who cares), threatening to call my mom (fine), and telling me there would be consequences for this. She got really animated about the whole thing. If I didn't know any better, I'd say J.T. looked practically embarrassed for her.

I just let her talk. It's not like I've never gotten yelled at like this before, so everything she said just kind of washed over me. If anything, I was relieved to be off the floor again, putting my painful past novel behind me.

We made our way back to the main building, and I saw Tony C. sneaking out a good distance behind us, totally unnoticed.

June is less into my belief in cosmic destiny than I am.

But get this: my punishment is to stay with the chaperones for the rest of the trip. First of all, that's fine because the trip is basically over, apart from the drive back home. And secondly, this means I get a full three hours of unrestricted access to my chaperone escort: *Gwen's mom.*

MISHA'S DIARY OF SITTING NEXT TO GWEN'S MOM ON THE BUS

0 minutes in.

Things are already going extremely well. When I got handed over to Gwen's mom outside the bus, I wasn't sure she'd remember me from the time she wrote me a note for being late to school, so I'd made up my mind to introduce myself boldly and confidently.

So she thinks I'm Bethany, which is my mom's name, but I think that's fine. Maybe "Bethany" can even be the pen name I use for our book. Reader, if you've been confused this whole time by why I was calling myself "Misha" instead of my famous name "Bethany," this was why. Now you know where it all began.

15 minutes in.

Things continue to go extremely well. She's been looking at her phone this whole time, but I can tell she thinks I'm mature and adult for not disturbing her and instead working diligently in this notebook.

I'm going to see if I can get her attention with some art on the next page. Not to show her the story (not until it's done, OBVIOUSLY), but just to get her interested. A sneak peek. The goal is to have her say something like, "Wow, you're pretty amazing at drawing," or "Tell me a little bit more about this character you've got," which I can use as an opening to get her hooked. Here we go . . .

LIGHT MAGE

30 minutes in.

The drawing on the last page hasn't worked yet, but I think it was because my positioning wasn't right for her to be able to see it easily.

BAD ANGLE:

IDEAL ANGLE:

I'm going to try in this optimized position to see if it's any easier for her to notice.

32 minutes in.

Things were going great with the new drawing position until Mike walked up to the front of the bus to get a bottle of water.

Hey Misha, you drawin—

thump
NOPE

45 minutes in.

Gwen's mom gets <u>a lot</u> of notifications on her phone, wow.

1.5 hours in.

I thought it might be a good conversation starter if I mentioned something from one of her videos, to show I'm a fan.

I looked up Clarista Stevens on my phone, and it looks like they're another famous person on the internet. Gwen's mom definitely still was the one who said the line I was quoting, even if I didn't get it 100 percent right.

2.2 hours in.

She asked me to pull down the blinds on our bus window.

2.4 hours in.

She asked me to raise the blinds again a little.

3 hours in.

We were supposed to be home by this point, but there was terrible traffic that took forever. I was pretty ready to be off the bus, when all of the sudden . . .

I was totally confused but did my best to hide it.

"You have to mess up if you want to get anywhere in life," Gwen's mom went on. "Take risks. Make mistakes. I'm always trying to tell Gwen this."

I bit the inside of my cheek.

"People always get mad at me when I take risks," I said.

"Maybe it's time to leave those people behind," she said back. It was like she didn't even have to think about it.

"I've had to reinvent myself over and over again," she said. "I've had to leave my old self behind. Every time I did, it was a risk. But every time I did it, it paid off."

Then she asked if I wanted a picture, and I said YEAH, obviously. She took it on her phone and texted it to me. There's a chance she might even post it on her account. Just think of what kind of amazing advertising that would be.

"Remember this," she said as she put her phone away. "Reinventing yourself is the key to being your authentic self."

I was awestruck.

"Be authentically you, Bethany," she said.

I felt 5 percent guilty, 95 percent awestruck.

We heard the sound of the bus grinding to a stop.

"Looks like we're here," said Gwen's mom. "Fun trip, buddy." She reached overhead and pulled a bag down from the racks above. Then, right before she stepped off the bus, she turned back to look at me one last time.

Nice drawings, by the way

I'll admit I was a little disappointed at how the trip with Gwen's mom had gone . . . up until that moment when it did a 180! I was so shaken up that I just sat there after, totally overwhelmed while everyone streamed past me to get off the bus.

And even though June told me it was weird, I still picked up the pieces of trash Gwen's mom accidentally left behind, so I can remember this day for all time. I'm going to staple them in here. After all, since Gwen's mom is the one who's going to get Deltovia published, she's as much of a part of this story as we are. Plus, it has to be a sign—that she has a bag that stuff sometimes falls out of, just like I do.

LAKEVIEW MALL

HOW'S OUR SERVICE?
Call 1-800-XXX-XXXX

3:22 PM
Store: 47451
Cashier: 25252000
SALE

PUMPKIN CHAI CANDLE $49.99
ARCHITECT VAN CNDL $24.99
FIG & LOTUS CANDLE $64.99
GINGER PLUM CANDLE $22.49
OLIVE ROSE CANDLE $29.99
LAVENDER ESPRIT CNDL $79.00
LATTE LOVE CANDLE $33.99

Subtotal $305.44
SALES TAX $15.27
Total $320.71

APPROVED
Payment Type: Credit
Credit Card 3929

CUSTOMER COPY

Anyway, I'm home now and I'm feeling unbelievably inspired. Going to get this down in writing while I'm riding this wave of creative energy.

CHRONICLES OF DELTOVIA: CHAPTER 25

The group was walking back from the Supreme Magical Circle, which everyone agreed had been a great place to get prophecies from and level up at. As they walked, Melodia felt an otherworldly being approach her from the side. She looked over and saw it was Gwelle's mom, the Mage of Light, who was very glowy.

"Chosen One," said Gwelle's mom. "I sense you understand what it means to leave the past behind and move forward for your goals."

"Yes," said Melodia. "I used to be super embarrassing, and I didn't know how the world worked. But now I'm jaded and wise."

Gwelle's mom nodded in understanding. "The Tome of Destiny was right to choose you," she said. Melodia humbly nodded.

"When we return to the school, you will face the Trials," continued Gwelle's mom. "These are a test that everyone has to do, but lots of people fail. The first one is the Trial of Wisdom. It is very hard and dangerous, but I know you can do it. It's critical to your destiny."

"The Trial of Wisdom . . ." Melodia thought, nodding to herself. She could tell she would be spending a lot of time thinking about that. It was critical to her destiny.

CHRONICLES OF DELTOVIA: CHAPTER 26

Actually, she didn't think of the Trial of Wisdom much at all because it was Winter Break at the Academy when they got back, and they had to celebrate the Winter Ritual and everyone got pretty busy with that.

114

December 22nd

OK, so I might have forgotten that right after the school trip, there were like five days before Winter Break, and I might have also forgotten to bring the notebook to school for those five days, and now we're on vacation and it's basically Christmas.

Don't worry though: I filled June and Ollie in on everything that happened during the trip at school, and they, like me, were pretty excited.

I told June about how Gwen's mom is even more sure to help us now, and she was like:

Misha, we only have one chance to go through middle school and make middle school memories together, and if we lose that chance because you get expelled, we'll regret it every single day for the rest of our lives.

I agree that things are looking good with Gwen's mom.

And then I told Ollie what happened, and she said:

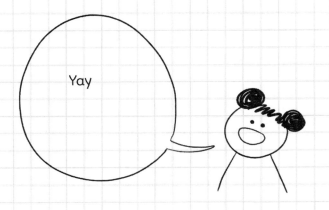

Yay

Then it was Break all of the sudden, and the teachers were all sending us home. Mrs. Hargrove didn't even give us homework to do. Mr. Nolan told us to have an excellent nondenominational time, which was probably a super funny thing to say if I knew what that word meant.

I saw Gwen on the last day before break as we were heading out. I almost went up to her to tell her that I talked to her mom, and more about the book in general, but she got away before I had the chance.

List of Things I Know about Gwen:
- Pretty good at camouflage

June is visiting her grandparents for the holidays right now, but we've been texting a lot. She sent me one picture of her family wearing matching Christmas sweaters and approximately 200 photos of "exceptionally interesting Scrabble games."

Ollie's still in town, and we walked over to the gas station the other day to get snacks and hang out. Ollie bought an entire loaf of bread.

For Christmas, I got my mom a cactus since she always jokes about killing plants, and the person said these were basically impossible to kill. I got my dad a funny picture I made on the computer of mashed potatoes on a snowy background, which is an inside joke between the two of us.

It basically looks like this:

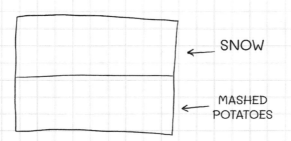

I'm going to stay up so I can email it to him.

December 27th

On the Christmas call with my dad, he said he loved my picture.

I am a gift-giving genius.

December 31st

For Christmas, I got lots of awesome things, but my favorite was a set of little candles that each have a different color. I lit one a few minutes ago so my room is spooky in a good way right now.

It reminds me a little of Gwen's mom's book's cover. That lady loves candles. I think she's even sponsored by some really fancy brands. But I like my candles better.

New Year's is weird. I get all lonely and quiet and I miss my friends really badly, but I also kind of want to be alone. It's probably a genius thing or something.

Anyway, I wanted to add one last chapter before the end of the year, so here we go.

CHRONICLES OF DELTOVIA: CHAPTER 27

Melodia, Jayana, and Ollie sat around the warm fire at the Deltovian Royal Academy Winter Ritual's Winter Feast. It had been four whole months since they first came to Deltovia and already so much had happened. As Melodia looked at her two friends, she knew she would do anything to defeat the Vile One and make them famous throughout the lands. And she also needed to figure out why she only had one wing. She was also definitely going to start thinking about the Trial of Wisdom pretty soon.

CHRONICLES OF DELTOVIA: CHAPTER 28

Jayana thought that a lot more background was needed for the reader about Deltovia. Deltovia has seasons, much like Earth, but there are six of them instead of four—spring is the same as Earth, but summer is divided into Epsosummer (a period marked by rapid thunderstorms that occur even though the sun is still out the whole time) and Lorosummer (when all the clouds are perfect circles), while fall is divided into Epsofall (same as Epsosummer, except instead of thunderstorms it's leaves falling from extremely tall trees) and Autumnio (sandstorms). Winter is the same. The Winter Ritual is a yearly celebration of the achievements of the previous year, with ceremonies such as The Awarding of the Gems and Certificates for Excellence and the lighting of the Thirteen Bonfires.

The Winter Ritual takes place in the Deltovian Royal Academy Circular Gardens. The twelve lesser bonfires are arranged around the center Prime Bonfire.

As she looked into the fire, Jayana knew that the trials ahead would be tough. She knew they might not make it. She thought about how you must treasure what you have, because good things are always gone too soon.

Ollie thought "_____Happy new year squad!!!!!_____."

January 6th

Dear Reader,

Misha, as you now know, has not been expelled, thankfully. But we cannot allow ourselves to become complacent. The Planetarium Affair, along with last year's Incident, has put her on thin ice.

Mostly, though, I'm relieved it wasn't worse. Misha does indeed have enemies at the school and, as I have already noted, she _does not_ think things through all the way. The whole reason The Incident happened was because Greg Janssen made her mad. She was not thinking about what would come after, nor was she planning ahead beyond proving Greg Janssen wrong.

It would be really, really bad if anything happened to her. Which is why I'm going to be extra sure to keep an eye on her in the new year.

Yours,
June

Dear Misha,

Thank you for remembering to bring the notebook back to school. As you will see when you reread the last chapter, I've added some more world-building and details for the reader. We will likely need six thousand times as much background detail of that kind in the final product.

Speaking of details, I have decided this year to help you stay on track, academically speaking. I know you do not always pay the most attention to detail in the assigned homework, but if you write down what you think the assignments are in here, I can double-check to make sure you've got all of them and help you to be sure to complete them all by the deadline.

Regards,
June

Dear Misha,

Just making sure what I just wrote doesn't come across as too stern or hurtful. Obviously, while I want you to succeed, I don't want to do it at the cost of our friendship. I would have edited my language some more, but, once again, I wrote it in pen.

Your friend,
June

January 7th

Hey girls!! Welcome back!!! Did you hear that Candace got her nose pierced over break?? I only saw it from a distance, but I think it looks GREAT.

Coach Kim told us at winter training yesterday that we're going to have a pep rally for the winter/spring sports in a week or so, AND that there's going to be classroom parties after to celebrate. Then she told us to always stay hydrated.

Too bad we're back at school (bleh) but so happy to see you two again!! Missed you!!!

January 8th

Ya guessed it, Reader: we're back in school. Back to this:

Nobody's exiting this space until I get an example of a simile

Some of this also:

LAPS
[but on the indoor track]

Not exactly the ideal environment for our untamable creativity, but we can work with it.

When my mom sent me off to school again, she was her normal not-at-all-sentimental self.

How about you let me buy you a new backpack, and we keep the old one in a dusty closet where no one can see it?

No!

A weird thing happened right before third period. I was at my locker, having a perfectly normal snack, when Tony C. came up to me.

Then he just kind of stood there without saying anything.

Then in third period, he actually moved his seat to be farther from me. Even though his normal seat is in the back by the window, one behind and one to the left of me, he moved to three behind and one to the left of me. Normally, I wouldn't say anything, but I thought it was weird, so I asked him about it.

Why aren't you in your normal seat?

He just shrugged and said, "Dunno."

Then he picked up his stuff and moved back to his normal seat without saying anything, and Mr. Nolan spent the class giving out candy to anybody who could still remember world capitals after break (I got six).

Which is just more evidence of the following: June, you don't have to worry about me. Trust me. I'm going to be just fine, school-wise. But just to put your mind at ease, here's everything I have written down in my planner as things I need to do:

GEOGRAPHY: no homework

ENGLISH: read *The Hobbit*

MATH: odd problems, pages 70—74

BIOLOGY: plant cell wall worksheet

DELTOVIA: write Chapter 29 and get one step closer to changing the world forever, along with getting one step closer to being extremely famous and world-renowned

What about the Earth Science quiz?

Earth Science quiz?

The one this afternoon?

. . . Earth Science quiz?

January 15th

So, I may have completely forgotten that we had an Earth Science quiz last week on chapters we were "apparently" supposed to "read" before the "break." In my defense, I was thinking about deeper, more meaningful things than "how does the ocean work," like "why does Melodia only have one wing" and "when will the secret of the Vile One be revealed" and "is it possible Mrs. Hargrove hid a body in the halls of our school forty years ago."

Anyway, while I didn't do great according to "typical" standards, I think I did pretty good for somebody who only found out about the test forty-five minutes ahead of time.

I mentioned something about my grade on the quiz to Ollie, and she was like:

Then I showed it to June and she was like:

No...oh no

Which is a silly reaction to have (no offense, June). Life's not about how you do in school; it's about what you do in the real world. And what we're going to do in the real world is become very genius superstar writers. Which is why we can't let ourselves fall behind on what's TRULY important:

CHRONICLES OF DELTOVIA: CHAPTER 29

Winter Break ended and it was time for the Trial of Wisdom. Melodia, Jayana, and Ollie made their way to the examination room, which was at the top of a spiral tower. There, waiting for them, was the Witch of Life, Doctor Pendletonth.

To pass this trial, you must impress me... with your minds!!!

(This staff is either brains or clouds, I can't decide)

The Trial of Wisdom, being the first of three trials, was designed to assess the knowledge and logical abilities of the students of

the Deltovian Royal Academy. It was extremely important for their success in the real world and as humans. If they didn't pass, their future opportunities would be limited, and they might even be expelled. It was an incredibly serious event.

Doctor Pendletonth waved her arms, and suddenly they were all in a giant purple bubble with pink dots floating in midair.

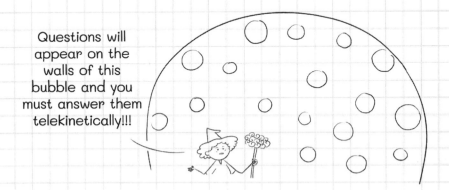

Questions will appear on the walls of this bubble and you must answer them telekinetically!!!

"This will be easy," Melodia thought.

"It will be easy IF we take it seriously," thought Jayana.

Suddenly, the trial began!

PEW
PEW
PEW

$2 + 2 = 4$

MIND ANSWERS

(Ollie, put stuff here:)

Answering
questions

Before long they heard a voice interrupting their demon-
strations of knowledge.

Congratulations.
You have now
passed the Trial
of Wisdom

"The next two tests are the Trial of Strength and the Trial
of Soul," she said. "These test your real-world skills, and you
definitely won't need to study for them or do anything like
that."

"Great," said Melodia. "Now there's no need for us to worry
about studying ever again."

January 22nd

I have agreed, at June's insistence, to try to do more studying. I am going to, as she has requested, keep her informed
of my homework in here so she can make sure I'm doing it,
even though there's basically no chance of me forgetting
something like the Earth Science quiz ever again. Here is
my homework for the week:

GEOGRAPHY: no homework

BIOLOGY: animal cell worksheet

MATH: Numbers 1—18 (even) on page 88; numbers 22, 23, 25 on page 89

EARTH SCIENCE: study for make-up quiz

ENGLISH: find book for book report

DELTOVIA: write Chapter 30 and get one step closer to changing the world forever, along with getting one step closer to being extremely famous and world-renowned

I solemnly promise I will be sure to do all of these things. No need to worry about me.

January 25th

Dear Reader,

My older sister was telling me about high school last night, and I have to admit, I was not particularly impressed with what she had to say. It sounds like middle school, except you're even less likely to have class with your friends, and some people can drive, except probably not very safely.

You still keep your old friends, but you make all new ones as well. It's all about finding yourself

I have already found myself. I am found.

You're comfortable right now. You need to broaden your horizons. Give up a little control

I don't need to do any such thing.

And then Misha tried to chime in from across the table, and I had to remind her that she could participate in the conversation when her extra credit project was done.

Friday was the winter sports pep rally. It was, shall we say, underwhelming. Ollie was great in it, of course, but the classroom parties that were supposed to happen afterward were almost nonexistent.

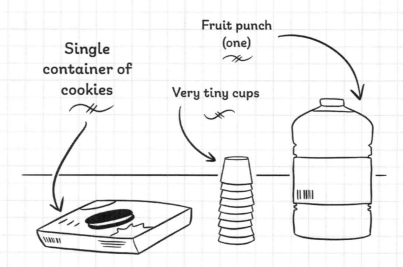

Single container of cookies

Fruit punch (one)

Very tiny cups

J.T. Fleet, as you could imagine, was not impressed.

I thought Tony C. might say something since he always seems to wake up when J.T. Fleet says something pretentious, but he was over by the window writing something and seemed not to notice.

I thought about saying something myself, but before I could:

I have to admit . . . I was impressed. I might have even snorted slightly. Discreetly. Candace is maybe the most popular girl at our school, but she isn't always friendly. At least she wasn't in elementary school. I'd always assumed she and J.T. Fleet were close since their parents are both highly active in the PTO, but it appears I was wrong.

It made me think that we should give Centipedia, and some of the other characters, more attention in the book. Other characters are part of the world-building, after all. Which reminds me: I've promised Misha she can have this notebook back when she's done studying, so I might as well use this time to clean up some loose plot holes.

CHRONICLES OF DELTOVIA: CHAPTER 30

Jayana sat down in the Grand Deltovian Library. Azariel walked in.

"Hello, Jayana. I wanted to let you know that I am still around—I just haven't been doing things in the same room as you, Melodia, and Ollie."

"That's good to know; thank you, Azariel," said Jayana.

Azariel said goodbye and left.

Centipedia and Graviton walked in.

"Hello, Jayana," Centipedia said. "Isn't it funny that just a few months ago we had that Battle Royale that, while seeming to pit us against each other, actually existed to bring us closer together through a shared experience, and all the people who appeared to die have in fact been resurrected by healing magic?"

"Very funny," Jayana agreed. Everyone laughed.

CHRONICLES OF DELTOVIA: CHAPTER 31

"How is your training going?" Jayana asked Centipedia.

Jayana thought often about all the training they had been doing. Even though it might have seemed like they were only doing exciting things like going to the Supreme Magical Circle and taking the Trials, lots of training was going on every day.

"I can now control all the bugs within a two-mile radius," Centipedia said. "My power is called insectopathy."

Jayana nodded. It was as she had suspected. She waved goodbye to Centipedia and Graviton and returned to reading.

She continued to keep her suspicions about the Vile One, which she still had and was certainly correct about, to herself.

February 6th

Hey girls!! I learned something awesome from Yvonne and Autumn!! Apparently there's going to be a DANCE in the spring that will have a raffle with prizes like a FREE MINI DEHUMIDIFIER in it. It's got an UNDER-THE-SEA theme!

Great chapter, June!! Let me know if there's any spaces I need to fill out in the next one!!

February 8th

We had to do work with partners in Geography today, so Tony C. and I decided to pair up. Geography is the only class besides homeroom where both June and Ollie aren't there, so I usually try to avoid eye contact with anyone until Mr. Nolan either lets me work solo or puts me as a third in a group of three, where I then proceed just to work solo. And by work, I mean "work on *Deltovia*."

But I think Tony and I have come to an understanding. We each let each other work on our own stuff, and neither of us asks questions. Tony has his own notebook to write in, and I have mine.

I'll admit, I am kind of curious what he is writing in there when he's not napping.

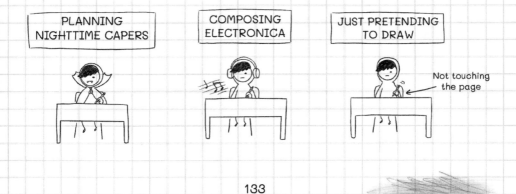

PLANNING NIGHTTIME CAPERS

COMPOSING ELECTRONICA

JUST PRETENDING TO DRAW

Not touching the page

Class was halfway over when Gwen walked in late. That's pretty common. I think it has to do with her mom being really busy and having to drop her off late because she's got so much going on. Mr. Nolan went ahead and put her in our group as the third person, and I saw my chance to make some ~~friend~~ acquaintance-style moves.

So, not a slam dunk, but still *progress*. I tried to see if I could get her to strike up a conversation by drawing some cool art, but she seemed really interested in the archipelago worksheet. And . . . kind of sad. Like usual.

I thought more about Mrs. Hargrove today after I walked past her room on my way to fourth period. She was reading a newspaper and looking at it intently. I mean, maybe she was just reading a newspaper. But it got me thinking.

Of all the teachers at our school, Mrs. Hargrove is definitely the one who's most capable of hiding a skeleton in the walls and getting away with it. She's really quiet, which means she can sneak up behind you in class without you realizing it. And she always points out ten billion details in the books we read, which means she's got an eye for detail, which is useful for leaving no trace when you're hiding a skeleton.

Something is definitely going on at the school. Not to be too J.T. Fleet or anything, but it is a little weird that things just aren't as nice around here anymore. Like at last year's pep rally party, we definitely had cupcakes. Teacher Appreciation Week was definitely pretty crappy this year. And I'm the last person to care about something like a dance, but didn't last year's have a free *bike* for the raffle?

Do you think she could be sabotaging the school to make it so they don't have any money left for building improvements? To keep us from discovering the skeleton she maybe hid in the walls somewhere? Should we go look at old newspapers in the library to see if any students disappeared around the time the last renovations happened? That's a thing people do, right?

Dear Misha,

But if she's taking money from the school, wouldn't that make people think we need more money, not less? And that we really need an improved school?

Sincerely,
June

Maybe Mrs. Fleet is the one who is pushing for the school to be renovated? After all, she seems to care so much about how our school compares to the private schools. Mrs. Hargrove could be trying to scare her off with bad party snacks so she moves J.T. to a private school and the project gets cancelled??

Just saying it's a possibility.

Great theories, you two!! I think you both might be onto something. You've got my vote!

CHRONICLES OF DELTOVIA: CHAPTER 32

Life at the school went on as normal.

But there was also something going on at the school that was extremely diabolical, and nobody seemed to notice.

Jayana definitely noticed, as she had been carefully analyzing everything that happened at the school since the first moment she arrived.

Jayana noticed, and so did Melodia and Ollie.

There was something off with the buildings at the Deltovian Royal Academy. . . something was haunting them. The Veil wiggled creepily in the breeze as they walked by it. The air was . . . creepy. One day, Melodia and Jayana and Ollie were walking by an especially old building and saw the Witch of Language emerging from it, reading a Deltovian newspaper and looking suspicious.

It was the Library of Forgotten Souls, which had a 10,000-year history that I will expand upon later.

Yes, and she looked super suspicious.

Ollie thought _____ it was fun to talk to animals _____.

Ollie actually hadn't unlocked the power of talking to animals at this point, because that prophecy hadn't been fulfilled yet, so she was thinking about how it *would* be fun to talk to animals when the prophecy got fulfilled in an epic way.

Jayana didn't think any of these prophecies were going to come true.

Melodia ignored them and looked at the Witch of Language . . . and a shiver went up her spine.

February 22nd

I had the most amazing idea the other night when June was making me review my planner for the eighth time. I knew I needed to pick a book for the book report, but which one? At first I thought *Deltovia*, but FIRST of all, we're still not done with it, and secondly, we might mention Mrs. Hargrove possibly hiding a skeleton in the walls at least a couple times.

Then it hit me. What better book to do a book report on than . . . GWEN'S MOM'S BOOK? This way, everything I learn from reading it will actually be useful in real life—namely, getting Gwen's mom to support us and help us publish *Deltovia*.

I dug out my copy of *Genevieve Unadorned* and flipped through it. I was looking for the thing Gwen's mom had told me about reinventing yourself. That had really stuck with me.

It wasn't in there, at least not on the surface. But you could get the message if you read between the lines. She talked about making unboxing videos, where she opened packages, and then DIY videos, where she made things out of other things. You could see how she reinvented herself over and over again, leaving the past behind like it was no big deal.

It makes me relieved to know that everybody has a *The Candelabra* in their past that they're trying to forget. Not <u>literally</u> *The Candelabra*, so replace that in your head with the actual embarrassing thing that haunts you to this day.

Everybody has their own version of this:

My true heart's wish is that everyone has a friend and no one has to be alone if they are sad!!!

But *Genevieve Unadorned* helped me realize that I can put that behind me and embrace my new self.

Ugh, Mike leaned over to ask me what I was working on, and I couldn't fully keep him from seeing that last drawing. I know he just does it to bother me, but I'll be the one laughing when our book comes out and we're very famous and on talk shows.

I want to thank Genevieve Rossi, for seeing the spark in us and giving us our big break

And I want to anti-thank Mike

Anyway, my book report will discuss this theme so well that I'll be sure to get an A, unless somehow Mrs. Hargrove senses we suspect her and decides to take a terrible vengeance on me.

March 1st

Dear Reader,

Our homeroom teacher, Mrs. Applebaum, was out today, so we had a substitute who let us do homework without requiring any kind of silence. I was thinking I might spend the time working on our book when a voice interrupted me.

I wasn't sure why Candace wanted to talk to me. I went back to writing.

I thought it mildly ironic that the person who spent most of elementary school loudly asking me why I was so quiet didn't even remember my name. I went back to writing.

You're friends with that girl who climbed on the roof last year, right?

I started coughing and didn't stop for three minutes.

When I finally managed to catch my breath, I asked her how she knew about that. She shrugged, then I asked her why she was asking, and she shrugged again. Then I told her I didn't see why it was so important since no one was hurt.

"I was just curious," she said with a shrug. Then, after a beat: "My dad said she could have fallen and killed herself and then the school could have gotten sued. "

I told her maybe the school _should_ have been sued for having old facilities where it was (and probably still is despite recent improvements) exceptionally easy to get on the roof.

I also assured her that Misha would never do something so reckless again, especially for someone who was _barely_ an acquaintance, like Lana M.

"OK," she said.

Dear Misha,

Candace's dad, who is on the Parent Teacher Organization board, is talking about you. This means the PTO is talking about you. You have to keep a low profile or you could get expelled, permanently! 95 percent chance!!

Yours cordially,
June

March 2nd

June, I think everyone at school probably knows about the thing with Greg Janssen.

Reader, it was stupid. Greg Janssen and his friends found this sketchbook that belonged to a girl named Lana who went to our school, and they threw it up on the roof. I went to go get it back, and when I came back down, I got in big trouble, and Lana M. didn't even care, and then she transferred to a different school.

I'm a lot smarter and cooler than I was then, and I wouldn't go out of my way for some random person anymore.

Plus, now I'm more acquainted with the real world. Humanity's dark side. Like, I was looking at the skeleton in Dr. Pendleton's class earlier today and thinking all about mystery and intrigue. I know it's only there because she teaches biology, but it had me thinking about deep stuff.

This time last year, it would have been a totally different story. I'm reinvented, and you don't have to worry about this kid.

March 3rd

Reader, there was a little more to The Incident than that.

Lana M. was something of a loner at our school. She kept to herself.

141

Nobody really knew much about her, except that she had a note-book she'd draw in. She seemed pretty protective of it. Misha decided she wanted to befriend Lana, since she seemed lonely.

It's the right thing
to do! It's...heroic!

So Misha started asking her to join us for lunch and seeing if she wanted to hang out with us outside of school. Lana M. never seemed to talk much. She seemed like she wasn't interested in engaging. I was wary, but Misha was determined.

We have to! Nobody should be without a friend!

Then one day, we were heading to the parking lot after one of Ollie's scrimmages, and we saw Greg Janssen and his friends laughing. When we got a little closer, we realized they were laughing at Lana M.

They had thrown her sketchbook onto the roof, like a Frisbee. Lana was just standing there. She didn't look upset or angry on the outside, just limp. But Misha became upset almost immediately.

Those jerks.

She was able to get to the ladder on the side of the building and climb up, thanks to the truly abysmal security the school had at that time. I watched her as she went and didn't say anything.

I was hugely relieved when she reappeared at the top of the ladder and climbed down right after, totally unharmed. I thought, like a fool, that we'd made it through the worst part. She looked so happy and triumphant as she handed the sketchbook back to Lana.

But instead of being glad that her book was back, Lana was . . . furious. She knocked it out of Misha's hands and started yelling at her.

She was so loud that it got the attention of a nearby adult, who came over and promptly learned from Greg all about Misha's rooftop visit. And Misha got in a lot of trouble.

I don't know what made Lana M. lash out at Misha and not Greg Janssen. I don't know why she was so angry.

But I do know we can't trust people we don't know.

Misha,

All I ask is that you're careful.

Yours,
June

March 3rd

HEY GIRLS!!! Wish me, Autumn, and Yvonne luck in the games this weekend!! We're gonna have some SERIOUS competition from Brookfield School. Coach Kim says SIX of them might make All-County!!!

Good luck, Ollie! I believe in you! I'm not worried about how you'll do, because I know you'll be fine!

Because there's NO NEED TO WORRY when everything is fine! And everything is fine with me.

Everything *might* not be fine with the skeleton that could potentially be hidden in our school. If we're going to worry about something, it should be that. I've decided to take the lead on cracking the case wide open.

I went to the school library to see if there were any old newspaper articles about people who got reported missing around the last time the school got renovated.

Gwen and her mom were in there talking to the librarian about something.

Sorry, that's just not the kind of thing that would get turned in to Lost and Found

Hate to say it, but it probably got thrown away

I didn't go up to them or say anything, since it seemed like Gwen's mom was pretty worried about the thing she'd lost. But I did make eye contact with Gwen for a brief moment. Once again, there was something about the way she was standing next to her mom that kind of reminded me of some-one, but I couldn't quite place it.

List of things I know about Gwen:
- Doesn't really smile, except in her mom's book's pictures
- Definitely reminds me of someone

After they left, I asked the librarian about the newspaper articles, and they just told me to check the county website, where there was absolutely nothing useful.

I wandered the shelves of books a little bit before I left, just in case there was any cosmic destiny moment that wanted to happen while I was there. Libraries have good energies for destiny. But nothing happened. Dud destiny day.

March 16th

Dear Reader,

Yesterday was the P.E. fitness test. While normally Misha and I have our place where we sit during gym whenever possible . . .

. . . today we were told that was not an option.

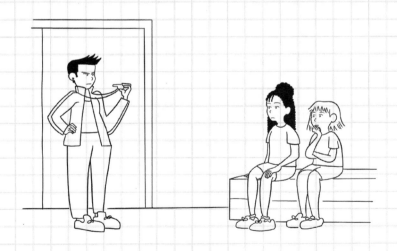

Ollie tried to help us make the most of it, but her words of encouragement could only help us so much.

You got this!!

Just a little more!!!

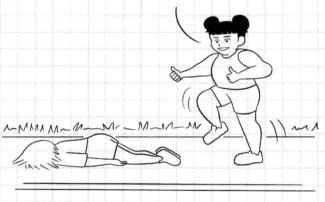

In the end, I was only able to pass the flexibility test. Misha, well . . .

I don't believe this will impede the development of our novel, but I do think Misha took it somewhat hard.

Misha,

Maybe we could start doing some jumping jacks each morning, as part of a training routine? We could do it on a video call.

Let me know if this would be something you'd be interested in.

Your friend,
June

I'd be down for that!!! What time do you two wake up????

March 17th

Whoa there. No need to make me do exercises. Now, it's been a day since it happened, but I remember the fitness exam *SLIGHTLY* differently than you do.

NOT TRYING VERY HARD   MERELY LOUNGING

   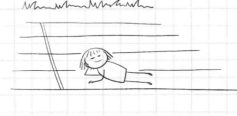

It didn't bother me at all not to "pass," because what really matters in life isn't how fast you can pick up a bean bag and turn around and bring the bean bag to a different location and then set the bean bag down and then go run back to get another bean bag. What matters is our art that is going to make us famous, recognized geniuses.

So I'm not about to let minor setbacks get under my skin. Relax, you two. Anyway.

CHRONICLES OF DELTOVIA: CHAPTER 33

It was time for the Trial of Strength, which everyone knew was the least important trial and the one that basically didn't matter.

Time to go, people!

Time to do a test that doesn't matter and isn't important!

The group headed down to the Field of Victory, where the assessment was to take place. The Field of Victory was named for the great battle that concluded there one thousand years earlier between the original Great Deltovians and the Titans.

Melodia was still recovering from her terrible injuries, but she summoned the strength to make a noble effort.

Ollie <u>did 10 x 2 min reps of sprints, 30 seconds rest</u> <u>in between, 45 minute jog</u>.

The battle between the Great Deltovians and the Titans was an epic fight that ended when the six High Houses joined forces to disassemble the Titans at a molecular level and spread their molecules around the globe. Every molecule became a Titan stone: the rare gems that cover the countryside, sparkling bright.

Ollie <u>did 4 x 20 seconds Mountain Climbers,</u>
<u>10 seconds rest; 4 x 20 seconds Donkey Kicks,</u>
<u>10 seconds rest; 4 x 20 seconds Jump Lunges,</u>
<u>10 seconds rest; 4 x 20 seconds High Knees,</u>
<u>10 seconds rest; 1 minute break</u>.

Melodia impressed everyone by persevering even though she was still recovering from her wounds and before they knew it:

EVERYONE PASSED

"Great," thought Melodia. "Now we'll never have to do any exercise again."

March 22nd

Ugh. My mom found out that I didn't pass the fitness exams and decided I need to start getting more exercise. So she's signing me up for SOCCER over the SUMMER.

It'll be fun!

Reader, the last thing I need is this taking up all my time over the summer that's supposed to be finishing up our book and maybe going on a book tour. I tried to reason with her, and she was TOTALLY unmoved.

I need to find some way to get her to care as much about my artistic soul as she does about my leg strength.

I'm in Geography right now, partnering with Tony on a Europe worksheet. We really do work pretty well together.

Worksheet

Just now, I looked over his shoulder at what he was writing in his own book. It was a drawing of a wizard guy, with tons and tons of details on it, who was super strong and cool looking. He looked basically like this:

That's incredible!

Thanks

We went back to working. Then a few seconds later:

I drew this guy on the bus this morning

He showed me an even more detailed wizard guy:

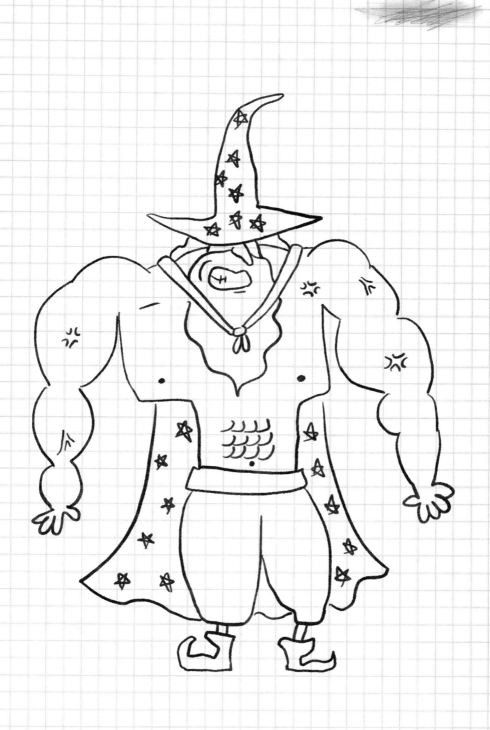

Then we went back to working.

It made me think we could really expand the role of some of the more minor characters to make our world fuller and more interesting.

CHRONICLES OF DELTOVIA: CHAPTER 34

Melodia was doing training meditation when Tonmy the Wind Mage walked by.

"Careful!" she said as he accidentally stepped below one of the psychic lightning diamonds she was levitating with her mind, even though she kept her eyes closed the entire time. "There are thousands of psychic lightning diamonds above your head."

"Cool," he said.

Tonmy used the powers of the wind to move out of the way of the psychic lightning diamond and levitated next to Melodia.

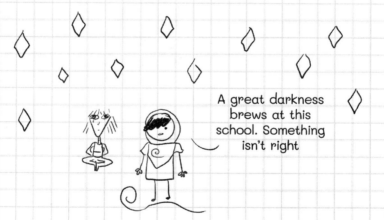

A great darkness brews at this school. Something isn't right

"I know," said Melodia solemnly. "And so does Jayana," she added before Jayana had to mention it.

"Indeed," said Tonmy, who was training to be a wizard and had his own stuff going on.

Behind them, a dark force slithered by, revealing that they were right—something very evil was going on.

March 24th

Because I live within walking distance from the school, I don't have to hurry out at the end of the day, though they still do a sweep of the school at 4:30 p.m. to make sure nobody's lurking. That gave me half an hour to investigate Mrs. Hargrove for suspicious activities. I just couldn't let her know I was on to her.

So I leaned casually against some of the lockers near her classroom, pretending to do math on my calculator. I would have much preferred playing on my phone, but I didn't want to risk having it taken away. Luckily, nobody bothered me or told me I had to leave.

When Mrs. Hargrove opened the door to her room and walked out, I was ready to silently follow. She was carrying something in her arms—a big sheet of paper.

I couldn't make out what it was when I was behind her, but I got a glance at it when I peeked out over the railing as she went down the stairs.

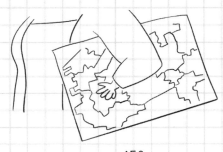

It was a huge map. I didn't recognize the lines on it at first. Then, as I sat and thought about what I'd seen, I remembered the shape the streets made from the time I'd mapped out the path from my house to June's. It was a map of our town, and there was a path drawn in highlighter on it.

What did she need that for? My mind raced as I quietly hustled down the stairs. Could she be planning to move the skeleton hidden in the school somewhere else before anyone else discovered it? Was that highlighted path her route?

I had lost track of her, so I put caution aside and burst out of the side doors to the parking lot, looking around to see if I could spot where she was heading.

Then I did a double take.

Right outside the door was Gwen, sitting on a bench, alone.

Normally I wouldn't do a double take at somebody sitting on a bench, but something was off. Gwen looks kind of down all the time, but today she looked . . . really, really down.

You...
OK?

I sat down next to her slowly. A couple seconds passed.

I can leave if you want

But...nobody should have to be alone...if they're feeling sad

We sat there a while in silence. Then, out of the blue:

What would you do if somebody you loved a lot was doing something they shouldn't, and they wouldn't listen to you?

Like, you're worried they're going to get in trouble?

Yeah.

I mean...sometimes you just have to let people do the things they want to do on their own—

—forget I asked.

Then she got up and started walking away.

I sat there, trying to process what had just happened for a second, and then, before I had figured it out, my legs started moving on their own.

"Wait," I said, chasing after her. "Hang on!"

She was far enough ahead of me that I couldn't really catch her without running, and I knew I couldn't run, or about half the stuff in my backpack would fall out through one of the holes.

But there was a path between the two of the trailers at the side of the school that I could take as a shortcut to catch up with her. I headed for the space between them, keeping my eyes locked on Gwen.

Which turned out to be a mistake, because:

TREACHEROUS PIPE

I looked like a total dork. Plus, as soon as I hit the ground, everything went flying out of my backpack through the one or two minor tears in it. It was a mess.

I lay on the ground and let my knee bleed. Gwen was long gone, and I'd somehow managed to make her upset with me.

I did have one good idea as I was lying there, though. My knee was scraped, but it wasn't enough to keep me from having to play soccer over the summer. But maybe I could somehow hurt myself more to get out of it. Like, if I fell out of one of the trees at school and broke my arm.

Anyway, I knew things couldn't get much worse.

CHRONICLES OF DELTOVIA: CHAPTER 35

Jayana went to Melodia's room.

"Melodia," she said, "It's very important that you're careful. Dark agents of the Vile One want to expel you from school."

"I promise I'll be careful," Melodia said. Then she went up into a tree and started practicing ways to fall and break her arm. "Ha, ha, ha!" Melodia said. "This is fun. I'd love to potentially injure myself and get expelled."

"Actually," said Melodia, "I didn't say that because the rule is that other people don't get to write characters that aren't their own. But I also won't actually hurt myself—that was just one idea to get out of something (namely, soccer) that was going to get in the way of us becoming famous heroes."

"Fine," said Jayana, who was (to be perfectly honest) still upset.

"Fine," said Melodia.

"Fine," said Jayana.

"Totally fine," said Melodia.

"SOUNDS GOOD TO ME!!!"—Ollie

April 1st

Reader, the bad times continue. First, we had some minor creative differences on *Deltovia*. Then I got my book report on *Genevieve Unadorned* back from Mrs. Hargrove. She gave me a C+. The comment at the top was: "Questionable choice."

Look, I know Gwen's mom doesn't write stories with plots or characters, and maybe her book is mostly photos, but my analysis of it was EXTREMELY deep. I included detailed write-ups on Gwen's mom's most popular videos. I included plots of her view counts! Mrs. Hargrove didn't care at all.

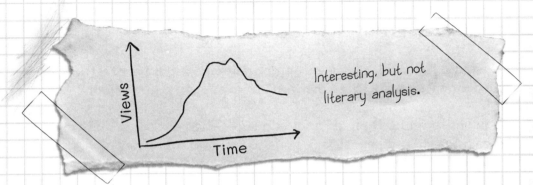

Interesting, but not literary analysis.

I was still grumpy about it in Geography class. Tony left me alone, and Mr. Nolan didn't call on me to name Canadian provinces. June didn't respond to any of the notes I tried to send her during Math class.

Ollie usually has practice after school these days, but the three of us used to go over to June's house after school all the time.

JOM Society is now in session!!

But I still go over to June's house all the time just to hang out and work.

Today I went straight home. I grabbed our book, dropped my backpack off inside the door, locked up behind me, and went to the little park over by my street. The one by June's house is nicer, so we used to play there more, but this one has got "being quiet and deserted" going for it.

I sat down on a swing and opened our book but couldn't think of anything to write, so I just sat and tried to come up with ideas.

It was really quiet, and the air was still a little cool, but there were little pockets of a warm breeze hitting my face. It was nice, and I had the sudden thought that I, alone in this park, on this swing, could be a cosmic destiny moment waiting to happen. I closed my eyes to better listen to any message the universe had for me.

Reader, Mike and I have known each other a long time. He's lived down the street from me forever. There were even times when he'd play with JOM Society back in the day.

But when we got to middle school, he'd started acting like he didn't even know me and started hanging out with Greg Janssen's crew. At the time, I didn't really know why he'd do that. Now I understood: he'd reinvented himself. Somehow, everybody is better at doing this than I am.

Yeah, I know. So you can make fun of it

No, I think it's cool you're writing a book... I've always wondered if you were going to finish that other one

I froze.

Which other one?

It was online. My mom showed it to me. I liked it, but you never finished it

WHICH. OTHER. ONE.

I think it rhymed with "beladabra"

I couldn't believe he knew about my embarrassing secret past. I couldn't believe he'd read it. I got up as fast as I could, ran home, and opened the website I'd posted *The Candelabra* on. I'd made it private a long time ago, but I

hadn't deleted it in case I wanted to look at it later. That ended today. I deleted it officially off the internet for good, and then I got in bed under all the covers. The Misha who wrote *The Candelabra* was officially dead.

April 5th

Reader, I'm in class right now, trying to get June's attention. We need to settle our creative differences. Right now.

June: see above.

Fine.

Fine.

Fine.

CHRONICLES OF DELTOVIA: CHAPTER 36

It was time for the Trial of Soul. The gang traveled to the place where it was going to take place: the Crystal Swamps.

Waiting for them there was the person who oversaw the Trial of Soul: the Witch of Language of the Deltovian Royal Academy.

So you think you've made it through the trials so far?

A dark aura filled the air, which was ominous and sinister. It was caused by the mildly toxic crystal blooms in the Swamps—geodes that bloomed into flower shapes and released a powdery dust into the air as they did.

"In this test," the Witch said, "I will look into your SOULS."

She looked into Melodia's soul, and she saw that she was dark and interesting and deeply afflicted by the suppressed memory of the mysterious injury to her other wing.

She saw that Melodia was jaded and strong and cooler because of it and the opposite of innocent and naive.

Then she looked into Jayana's soul and saw she had a tendency to worry about things she didn't need to worry about.

Then she looked into Ollie's soul and—

She went back to Melodia's soul. "I see you have a great bond with your friends," the Witch of Language said. "But I notice you also have a tendency to be (and I don't mean this to be harsh) extremely stupid and reckless."

Then she looked at Jayana's soul and said, "Just like your soul worries about trying new things. You are both about the same. Equally fine souls."

"Except your (Melodia's) soul causes pain and concern to your friends, while her (Jayana's) soul only wants to protect her friends."

Melodia doesn't care about ANYTHING but the FEW PEOPLE who are her friends.

No, she ALSO cares about: 1.) putting herself in danger, and 2.) chasing after Gwelle.

Why bring Gwelle into this?

Melodia only cares about taking care of her friends, but she's *so* eager to add Gwelle to the mix?

As an ACQUAINTANCE! To HELP us!

What if we're good enough on our own, without her? What if all we need is the three of us, and you're putting it all in danger by taking stupid risks?

Well MAYBE I

Dear Reader:

Some updates for you.

In the middle of working on that last chapter of *Deltovia*, June and I were interrupted.

No distractions in class.

I'll be taking this

It was not ideal, to be sure. June took it especially bad.

But it got worse when we went up to her after class to ask for it back.

I'm going to keep it a little longer. You may have it back when I'm done

Which was extra not-ideal since the story isn't complete yet.

And we may have something in there about her hiding a skeleton in the walls of our school.

June won't even talk to me about it. I think she might be too mad at me.

And Ollie's out with sports friends right now.

But I'm writing things down on these so you, our reader, can follow along.

And I'll stick them in the notebook once I get it back

That's right. I'm getting it back, even if I have to do it myself.

But first:

CHRONICLES OF DELTOVIA: CHAPTER 37

The reason the last chapter ended so fast was because shadow forces swarmed over Jayana, Melodia, and Ollie in the middle of the Trial of soul.

The Tome of Destiny was stolen from them!!!

Melodia awoke in the darkness and knew it was all up to her . . .

To defeat The Vile One once and for all . . .

April 5th

Strap in, Reader. Lots to catch you up on.

I went home yesterday determined to walk back to the school at night and sneak into Mrs. Hargrove's room and get our book back. I put on an all-black outfit to be more stealthy. My mom wasn't back from her shift yet, but I left her a note saying I was going to Ollie's and headed out alone.

Of course, I wasn't heading to Ollie's. I was heading to our school.

It's about an eight-minute walk from my house, but I took a stealthy path to approach from the back.

CAMOUFLAGE

I made it to the door by the band room and gave it a tug. It was locked.

Then I went around to the doors to Hallway C. Also locked.
Then I went around to the back door of the gym. Locked.

I was on the verge of needing to come up with a totally new plan when I heard voices behind me and ducked behind some bushes.

As the voices got louder, I realized who it was.

Why they couldn't let us
start setting up sooner,
I DON'T understand

SUPER JANGLY KEYS

All at once, I remembered. Tonight was the Under-the-Sea Dance. Mrs. Fleet and J.T. and whoever else was planning it were setting up.

She opened the door, and I waited as they disappeared into the gym and came out a few minutes later, arms empty.

The second they were mostly back to their car and out of sight, I snuck in through the now-unlocked door.

I was in. Next stop: Mrs. Hargrove's classroom. I stealthed up the stairs to the second floor where her room was and peeked down the hallway. It was dark.

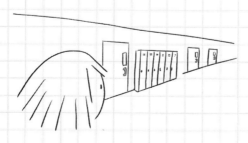

There was a jangling noise to my right, so I ducked back and counted to ten, then I poked my head out again.

Even though Mrs. Hargrove's hallway was dark, the hall that intersected it was not: The classroom lights were on, and the doors were propped open with chairs. There was a big cart in the hall.

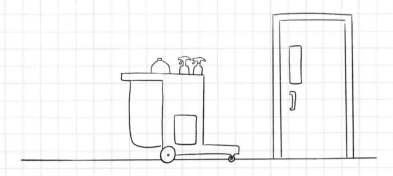

I didn't understand what was going on until the jangling noise happened again, and I saw Mr. Tranh, the janitor, making his way out of one room and into another.

He was going through all the rooms and leaving them propped open as he did. And if he was on that hallway now, he'd probably get to Mrs. Hargrove's soon. I darted across the hall junction and made my way to right outside Mrs. Hargrove's classroom . . .

. . . confirmed it was locked . . .

. . . and slipped into the single-stall bathroom that was conveniently right across from my target.

My plan? Wait until Mr. Tranh opened all the doors in *this* hall to clean them, slip into Hargrove's room while he was in a different one, and then make my grand escape.

Reader, it was so boring. I sat on the cold bathroom floor and imagined playing checkers on the tile. I couldn't watch any videos on my phone because I didn't have headphones. I would have sworn I had been there for two hours when I checked and saw it had only been thirty-five minutes.

In my head, while I was waiting, I wrote another chapter of *Deltovia* which I'll reproduce here.

CHRONICLES OF DELTOVIA: CHAPTER 38

Melodia was alone. After the darkness swarmed over her, Jayana, and Ollie at the Trial of Soul, she'd woken up and known she alone had to defeat the Vile One. But how could she do it without the Tome of Destiny? Her single demon wing ached terribly. She was all alone.

Suddenly a realization hit her: she wasn't missing a wing. She had only ever had one wing. Her single bat wing was a simile for her. It was all by itself in the world.

She needed to steal the Tome of Destiny back. If she could just get the Tome, she could use it to defeat the Vile One all by herself. She didn't need help from anyone else. She had to leave the past behind.

(Still April 5th)

After what felt like an eternity but was allegedly closer to two hours, I heard the sound of keys and the click-slide of doors being unlocked and propped open one by one.

They were getting closer to my hiding place in the bathroom. Soon, Mrs. Hargrove's room would be opened. I was a little nervous, but I mostly felt relieved that my plan was going to work.

Then it occurred to me that if Mr. Tranh was cleaning the whole hallway, he was probably going to clean the bathroom, too.

I had about 0.2 seconds to jump up, get flat against the wall behind the door, and hold my breath before he swung the door open.

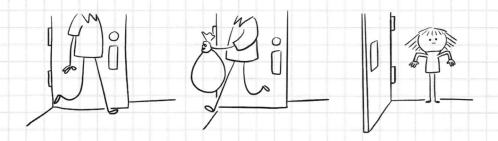

I listened as he finished going down the hall, then as he went back to where he started and into a room. It was time.

Stepping AS QUIETLY AS POSSIBLY COULD, I crossed the hall into Mrs. Hargrove's office and immediately started hunting for the notebook. My heart was pounding.

There was nothing on her desk. Nothing on top of the filing cabinet. Then I looked down at my feet.

There, tucked into a tote bag along with some other books, was *The Chronicles of Deltovia.*

I grabbed it and shoved it up my shirt. Then I peeked into the hallway one more time. There was no way to go back out the way I came without risking Mr. Tranh seeing me, but I could try heading in the opposite direction and hoping he didn't come out of a room and see me.

I took a big gulp of air and charged into the hallway, stepping as silently as humanly possible. I was almost to the stairs at the other end when I heard a loud clanging, thump noise, like something big had just gotten knocked over at the far other end of the hall. I abruptly turned left and ran as fast as I could down that hall, hoping desperately that Mr. Tranh wasn't right behind me.

I made it to the end, ducked into the stairwell, and focused on breathing for thirty seconds while I listened for the sound of footsteps behind me. I didn't hear anything there. Below me, there was some kind of low, bass sound, and it took me a moment before I realized the dance must already have started while I was hiding in the bathroom. I was hearing the music from a distance, muffled through the gym doors.

If I could just make it into the gym, slip into the crowd, and sneak out the door I came through, I'd be home free.

For the first time since losing the notebook, I started to feel something like relief. I walked down the first set of stairs and rounded the corner.

There was a person sitting on the stairs, near the bottom.

It was Gwen's mom.

Party's down here, buddy.

I knew I had to think fast.

I, uh, was using
the bathroom

She raised an eyebrow.

"Too good for these?" she asked, pointing to bathrooms that
were literally eight feet across the hall.

I......uh.....

"Relax," she said, looking at her phone. "I won't tell on you.
Just get back in there with your friends."

I was so close to being home free. I was almost past her
when:

Thanks, I—

In my defense, I had just sprinted like 150 feet and was kind of sweating a lot.

...What's that?

It's a book! A book I wrote with my friends

A book...

We were actually going to bring it to you, or Gwen, or you via Gwen when we're done with it. To get published

We have a cover letter

"What was that stapled in there?" Gwen's mom asked.

"Oh, uh—" I replied. "It's from the time you and I sat next to each other on the bus. It was on the floor, and I saved it. I guess you could say I'm a super fan. I wrote a whole book report abou—"

"You know, Bethany," said Gwen's mom, cutting me off. "I'd *love* to read that book of yours."

"REALLY???" I calmly replied.

All the stress of the last forty-eight hours was suddenly replaced with excitement. I couldn't believe my ears.

Then I paused. It was weird. I was about to achieve all my wildest dreams, but instead of thinking about a fancy house or the big, fancy armchair I was going to buy, I thought about June. I based a lot of *The Candelabra* on young me and June.

I took a few steps back. Gwen's mom got up from the stairs.

"I need that book, Bethany," she said. She sounded *deadly serious.*

I took a few more steps back, but I was kind of shaky still from all the running and sneaking, so I tripped and landed on my butt. Gwen's mom kept walking toward me. I was really starting to worry, when all of the sudden the door from the gym opened.

Hey Mish-Mash, why aren't you in here with the rest of your crew?

Relief washed over me.

"Mr. Nolan—" I began.

"Matthew," interrupted Gwen's mom. "She's taken a notebook of mine. I let her borrow it, but she won't give it back now."

I couldn't believe what I was hearing. The thought of this notebook being anything but ours was completely ridiculous! I turned to Mr. Nolan, expecting him to laugh her off, especially since I spent most of his class writing in our notebook anyway.

Instead:

Mr. Nolan reached out to try to grab the notebook, but I shimmied away with my shimmying skills and he missed me. I looked back at him and at Gwen's mom one more time.

Then I ran.

My first thought was that if I could just get into the gym, I could get lost in the crowd and disappear that way. But Mr. Nolan had been blocking the one entrance inside the school that led to the gym that I knew for sure would be unlocked. I didn't want to lose any time trying a door that I wouldn't be able to open. I was also pretty tired and didn't know how long I could run for. I needed a place to hide.

I ran down the hall that led to an exit outside and dived into the bushes as soon as I was out.

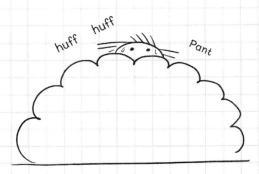

huff huff Pant

Mr. Nolan and Gwen's mom came out right after me, but they didn't see me. They slowed to a walk and started heading out into the parking lot. While they were looking that way, I slipped out of the bushes, back inside and up the stairs.

I was back on the second floor, which meant capture by Mr. Tranh was a potential hazard again. But the hallway I was in was totally dark, which I took to mean he'd started and finished cleaning it sometime in the three hours I'd been stashed in the bathroom in Mrs. Hargrove's hallway. The doors were almost certainly all locked.

But unlike *that* hallway, *this* hallway had the big sheet of plastic that blocked off the construction area. The Veil.

I jogged as fast as I could to the plastic sheet, lifted up the bottom corner, slipped into the darkness on the other side, and slammed straight into June.

For a second, June looked like she might die of shock.

She looked like this:

I, however, looked super confident and cool.

Dear Reader,

She looked like this:

From another angle, I looked like this:

CONSTRUCTION BOX

"June," I gasped, coolly. "What are you doing here?"

Dear Reader,

When our book was taken, I expected to have the normal thoughts I have when Misha is in danger. Namely:
-   **Is she going to be suspended?**
-   **Is she going to be expelled?**
-   **Will we not get to go to high school together?**

- Will we slowly drift apart, until we've forgotten we were ever friends in the first place, over the course of the long, long years?

But this time, something was different. I still was worried about Misha, but I was also still annoyed at her. And because I was annoyed at her, I didn't think:

It's up to me to save her. If I do not help my friend, she will get kicked out of school and forget how to read

Instead I thought:

She'll have to DEAL WITH THIS HERSELF

That feeling caught me off-guard, but the more I thought about it, the more convinced I became I was right. Misha always just *decided things* without caring what effect it had on me. Why couldn't I just decide to let her deal with her own problems?

But then another thought came to my mind. A memory. It wasn't about Misha.

It was about Candace Mitchell, two weeks ago.

You really like
doing that, huh?

Yet my words felt hollow as soon as they left my mouth. Not the "end in disaster without me" part, of course— that was still right. But something about what I'd said didn't feel right.

With the book in Mrs. Hargrove's hands, I realized what that feeling had been. I was writing our book because . . . I loved it.

I'd poured so many thoughts and ideas into it. It *really* was shaping up to be a masterpiece.

And I wanted it back, to see it to the end.

There was also a 0.5 percent chance Mrs. Hargrove would find something in the book that could get me into trouble, though I highly doubt it.

So I decided I would rescue the book on my own, even if my plan was—and I know this is a strong word to use, but it's accurate—haphazard. I put on an all-black outfit to be discreet. I felt a newfound electric energy course in my veins.

Unfortunately, I have to get a ride to school because it's too far to walk, so I couldn't begin the operation until I got my dad to drop me off.

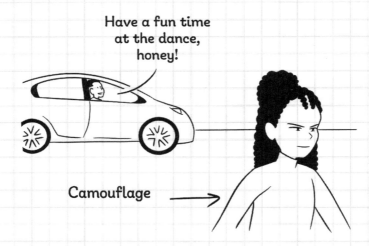

Have a fun time at the dance, honey!

Camouflage →

Instead of going into the gym where the dance was taking place, I snuck up the stairs near the entrance when no one was looking. I heard a jangling of keys. Mr. Tranh was cleaning Mrs. Hargrove's hallway on the second floor, and all the doors were propped open. I needed to make sure he was distracted before I snuck into her room to look for the book. Then I saw the skeleton in Dr. Pendelton's room.

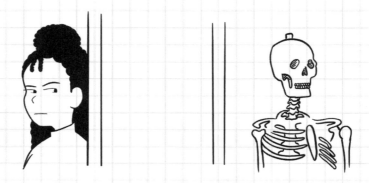

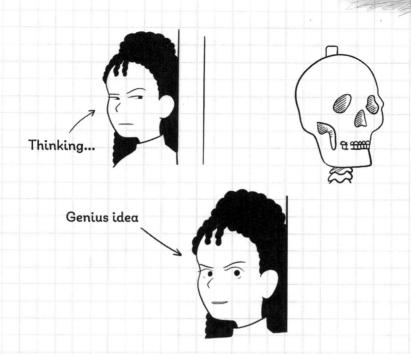

Thinking...

Genius idea

I rolled the globe from Mr. Nolan's room at it and knocked it off its pedestal.

It made an enormously loud clattering noise, and I watched from Mr. Nolan's room as Mr. Tranh walked into the classroom to see what had caused the ruckus. While he was distracted there, I snuck into Mrs. Hargrove's room.

But once I was in, I couldn't find the book anywhere. Not on the desk, not on the file cabinet, not in the tote bag on the floor near the desk. The whole time I was searching, I was mindful that Mr. Tranh could come in at any moment.

Eventually, I could tell I wasn't going to find it before he found me. It must have been in one of the locked drawers, or she took it home with her. I slunk back out into the hall when I could tell he was just starting in on a new room. The electric energy was leaving me. I needed a place to think. I remembered the construction area and ducked beneath the plastic sheet.

It was eerie and dark, and the air was stale, but my risk of discovery was low. I just needed a few minutes to collect my thoughts.

I'd been there for two minutes exactly when Misha flew through the plastic and squashed me.

"I couldn't find it," I whispered to Misha. "It wasn't in her class-room."

Then Misha smiled and pulled the book out from under her shirt.

"I got it," she said.

Suddenly, my (Misha's) phone started ringing. I looked down and tried to silence it, but I was garbage at finding the off button.

TRAITOR

Down the hall, we could hear Mr. Nolan's voice.

"Handy that you've got her phone number," he was saying. "Is that because she's a friend of Gwen?"

It was because of that photo we'd taken on the bus. She'd texted it to me so I could have a copy. I would have smacked myself in the forehead if I weren't so busy mashing the buttons.

"—did you hear that?"

I managed to put the phone on silent, but the footsteps were heading straight toward us. Our location had been revealed.

"We can hand ourselves over," I told June.

"No," I said. The electric energy was back. "We run."

The bottom corner of the plastic was flung upward, but June and I were already charging forward, out and underneath Gwen's mom's arm, running as fast as we could. From the corner of my eye, I could tell she looked furious.

Running was still pretty tough.

If I get through this, I will go to soccer camp and I will like it. I will run ten thousand laps. I will get super good at laps

But we beat them to the stairs, taking them like six at a time, and charged into the gym, where the dance was taking place.

All at once we were surrounded by people and sounds. The lights

were discoing above us. We waded through the people, hoping to use them as shields to block us from our pursuers.

In front of us, we spied Ollie. She was wearing a bright pink dress and standing in a group of athletic looking girls.

I said, "Hiii!!!!!"

"Ollie," I said, handing her the somewhat sweaty book. "Hide this somewhere. Take it! They don't know to suspect you. We can't keep going. You're our only hope."

K

We were about to turn around and start casually limping our way to the exit, when the overhead lights came on and the music cut out.

Sorry to interrupt the party, kiddos. We're looking for June Okoro and Misha Schmidt. Are June Okoro and Misha Schmidt in the gym today?

One hundred heads turned to face us all at once. Around us, the crowds parted, until there was a big, empty path between Gwen's mom and us.

"Give that book to me," she said, looking us dead in the eyes. We stood our ground.

Mrs. Fleet forced her way out of the crowd and started huffing toward us.

Gwen's mom kept stalking our way. Mr. Nolan trailed behind her, looking a little uncertain.

But I was surprised. Some other people pulled out of the crowd, too.

Gwen's mom was really close now. She made a swipe to grab it away from Ollie.

"Ollie!" June yelled. "Keep it away from her!"

Ollie immediately chucked it like a Frisbee straight into the crowd. It soared through the air. It went super far.

I saw sets of hands reach out to grab it, but I didn't see who ended up catching it.

Then I turned back to Gwen's mom.

"You won't get it back now," I said. "It's gone forever."

"Not quite," came a voice from behind both Mr. Nolan and Gwen's mom. I froze.

I also froze.

Yup.

Mrs. Hargrove was walking toward the center of the gym. At some point, she must have been up to her room, because she had the tote bag I'd stolen the book from around her shoulder. I paled.

I, too, was certain this was the end.

Yup.

I did have a chance
to photocopy your
receipts, Genevieve

Gwen's mom went super still. She didn't even look like she was breathing.

Then, almost as though she thought none of us would re-member how she had been acting for the last half hour, she laughed and flipped her hair.

At first: **Then:**

Marcia, I can honestly say I don't know what you're talking about

Marcia, really. Is this about Prop 12 *again*?

It's about the money that's been disappearing from your club, Anne

Mrs. Fleet looked angry and puffed up, and then she looked at Gwen's mom for back-up. But something she saw on her face must have thrown her off, because she got really still and quiet, too.

At that point, a lot of chaperones started making their way over, and the gym became loud again as everyone started talking and whispering to each other. It all became a bit of a blur, but we were ushered over to the side by Coach Kim and told to stay put while Mrs. Hargrove, Mrs. Fleet, Gwen's mom, and a couple of the other teacher-chaperones had some kind of discussion out in the hall near the gym. It went on like that for another five minutes, before one of the parents came in and awkwardly turned the lights back off and told the DJ they could play music again.

The DJ tried his best to get people to start moving again, but everyone was mostly standing around in circles, talking. A few people came over to ask us what was going on. Nobody came forward to hand us back the notebook that Ollie had thrown so athletically into the crowd.

I was relieved that Gwen's mom didn't get it, but still sad. I imagined Greg Janssen and his friends tearing out the pages one by one, or reading the pages out loud and laughing, or making a whole big deal about how it wasn't done yet.

Don't worry

When my dad arrived to pick me up, I half-expected to be forbidden to leave, but Coach Kim just kind of shrugged and gestured toward the door with her head. I asked my dad if he could also give Ollie and Misha a ride home, even though they live close,

because it was so dark outside, and he said, "Of course! Safety first."

We walked out the door and were almost to June's car when two super tall girls in floor-length dresses called out to us from the gym entrance. They looked vaguely familiar. Ollie waved at them like she'd been expecting them, and we walked back to meet them halfway.

I think this is yours

You didn't read it?

Ollie told us how important it is to you that it be finished before anyone else sees it

But based on what we've heard so far, it sounds really good

Can't wait to learn the secret of Melodia's missing wing

We headed back to the car. I'll admit I was very slightly shell-shocked. Behind me, Ollie waved at the two girls and said, "Bye Autumn! Bye Yvonne!"

When I got home that night, my mom was pretty close to being frantic.

Why didn't you pick up when I called?

I was so fried at that point I didn't even have the energy to explain that I'd put my phone on silent while trying to keep myself from being discovered by my classmate's mom and my Geography teacher. So I just apologized and said I had a good time at the dance and passed out facedown on my bed. She found out the rest of it later.

The next Monday, I went back into school and brought the notebook tucked safely in my backpack. I knew June, Ollie, and I had a lot of writing and catching up to do at lunch.

But before lunch, we had Mrs. Hargrove's English class. And sure enough, she told us to stay after class.

Miss Misha, Miss June: Certain facts lead me to believe that you may have done something you shouldn't have prior to the dance on Friday

But Mr. Tranh assures me that he saw no signs of anyone upstairs when they should not have been, apart from one strange incident with a globe and a skeleton

Yet you shall still face the consequences of your actions, I'm afraid

Then she handed us a sheet from a memo pad with writing on it, which I'm stapling in here so we don't lose track of it. There might actually be (don't get me wrong, I still don't know about her) some kind of helpful stuff in there.

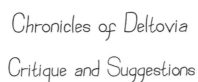

Chronicles of Deltovia

Critique and Suggestions

— In general, more showing and less telling would be helpful. Yes, Melodia is a tragic orphan, but this can be shown through her actions. Show her being slow to trust, for example.

— Excellent depth of world-building, though be careful not to let the details of the world overshadow the emotional throughlines.

— I'm intrigued by the character of Ollie, and I'd like to hear more from her. What's her motivation?

AND TO BE CLEAR: she also gave us detention right after. June looked like she was going to die, but I thought it was kind of a relief to see Mrs. Hargrove was the same as ever.

On our way to lunch, we passed Gwen in the hall, but she walked right past us like we weren't even there. I probably shouldn't have been surprised by that. There's been a lot of stuff that's come out just over the last weekend, and Gwen's mom isn't on the PTO anymore. Not to mention, we know why things at the school were going the way they were going.

April 8th

Last night I did a call with my dad. He even got to use the video kiosk for it, so we could see each other for once. I told him all about what went down. He knew some of it from my mom.

I hear there's a mom at the school who was doing a little fraud on the side, huh?

A FAMOUS mom. Who CHASED us

"So you and your friends brought down the bad guy, huh?" he asked.

"Yeah," I said. "I mean. Basically. It was . . . complicated. I think her channel wasn't doing as well as it used to."

He said all the dad-ly things he always does. Proud of me. Etcetera.

Then at the end of the call:

After we hung up, I lit one of my colorful candles and got on my computer to look up Gwen's mom's video channel again. Instead of sorting the list by "Most Popular," like I'd done in the past, this time I sorted from "Oldest to Newest" instead.

Her oldest video on the channel was only from a couple years ago, and I knew she'd been making videos since long before then. So then I searched for her account name and "deleted," and I found the old videos she'd taken down on another website.

She looked a lot younger in them but way more noticeable than that was the video quality. The lighting was pretty low, and the sound faded in and out. She was doing skits where she pretended to be two different people having conversations, and the pacing was a little slow. These weren't the videos that had made her famous.

But they actually were pretty funny. I started laughing by myself in my room at one of them. She seemed like the kind of person who might be a pretty fun friend.

I shut my laptop with a click and pulled a photo up on my phone. I'd known for a while who Gwen always reminded me of. Her mom reminded me of someone, too.

April 10th

Dear Reader,

It has been a stressful couple of days, but I am pleased to report that we have made it through. Misha is completely wrong that I was distressed by our detention from Mrs. Hargrove. The new, relaxed me is unfazed by that sort of thing. Any stories you may have heard about me trying to bargain out of it with promises of extra homework were exaggerated.

This notebook is almost out of pages, which I admit, I only gave us a 95 percent chance of achieving when we set out. But I believe there's still room for at least one more chapter to fit.

CHRONICLES OF DELTOVIA: CHAPTER 39

Melodia moved through the darkened campus of the Deltovian Royal Academy alone, trying to find the Tome of Destiny. She thought she needed to find it, by herself, if she wanted to save the world. She thought she needed to leave the past behind.

And yet, every path she took seemed to end in more darkness. She was going in loops, and she couldn't see a way out.

Suddenly, she thought back to the time back on Earth when Grog, who was then known as Greg Janssen, had thrown the sketchbook of a girl named Lana M. up on the roof.

Melodia had been very excited about being a hero. She'd climbed the ladder leading up to the roof, grabbed the sketchbook, and come back down again with it tucked under her chin, expecting to be greeted with cheers.

She'd wanted to help Lana, but more than that, she'd wanted Lana to help her be a hero. Kind of . . . as . . . a prop.

And when she'd come back down from the roof, she'd been surprised.

As she remembered that day, Melodia felt awful and embarrassed all over again. She felt like she was the worst.

And then . . . new memories crossed her mind.

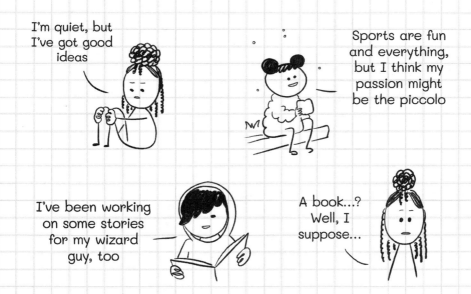

I'm quiet, but I've got good ideas

Sports are fun and everything, but I think my passion might be the piccolo

I've been working on some stories for my wizard guy, too

A book...? Well, I suppose...

She remembered all the times people had surprised her before. People surprised her all the time, because people were deep and complicated, and you couldn't just put them into roles or expect them not to change. Her old self had been complicated. A little corny, sure. But complicated.

And if bad surprises came from people being complicated, good surprises came, too. She remembered how her friends surprised her by staying by her side, even when she thought she was the worst. They were with her now, too, she realized.

Melodia snapped out of the curse that the Vile One had put on her. The dark miasma around her disappeared and she found herself on the Field of Victory.

To her left was Jayana, who transforming hydrogen and oxygen into a gigantic fireball.

I cannot transform this fireball into something more awesome

And to her right was Ollie.

In front of them was Gwelle's mom, holding the Tome of Destiny in her hands.

All around her, she saw her fellow students fighting to help get back the Tome.

Attack, my bugs!

Not everyone was helping. Like these two weren't:

But a lot of people were. It filled Melodia's spirit with a long-lost feeling. She was still cool as she did this, but her heart started to open up again. In a very cool way, she glowed and was lifted up into the air, and when she came back down, there was an angel wing across from her bat wing on her back.

HISS

Before long, Ollie saw her chance to strike:

Go animals!!!

Nooooo

The Tome was saved, and the Mage of Light collapsed to the ground.

It looked like it was over.

But was it *really*?

CHRONICLES OF DELTOVIA: CHAPTER 40

It was really over.

"The Mage of Light was corrupted by the Vile One," explained the Witch of Language, as the students stood amid the wreckage on the field.

"My dad told me she was stealing from the Academy's PTO," explained Centipedia. "Or at least using the money to buy things, and then returning them. Except she couldn't always get a full refund, especially if she lost the receipts. So the charges started to add up."

"Gwelle knew," said Melodia. "I think she didn't want it to happen, but she didn't want to get her mom in trouble either."

Jayana nodded because she had also figured this out.

"Yup," said Ollie.

"I shall say my farewells for now," said the Witch of Language, but before she left, she gave them a small nod.

They were surrounded by their teammates, and Melodia had one demon wing and one angel wing, because she was half-psychic-lightning angel, and half-psychic-lightning demon, and had embraced her dual nature. All was well.

"By the way," Melodia asked. "Does anyone know what the Witch of Language was actually trying to do if she wasn't trying to keep us from finding a body in the buildings of the Royal Academy?"

"Someone did mention something about Proposition 12," Jayana noted.

Oh, the school lines thing.

School lines thing?

They're going to change the school boundaries to change who goes to what school. We might have a totally new class next year.

"Now everything makes sense," said Melodia, finally at peace.

Wait.

What?!

ABOUT THE AUTHOR

Olivia Jaimes is a pseudonymous author and illustrator who has earned critical acclaim from *NPR*, the *New York Times*, the *Washington Post*, *Publisher's Weekly*, and many other publications. Jaimes is the first woman to write and illustrate the syndicated comic strip, *Nancy*, which appears in newspapers across the United States. She has authored two books, *Nancy: A Comics Collection* and *Nancy's Genius Plan*, both available from Andrews McMeel Publishing.

Andrews McMeel Publishing
a division of Andrews McMeel Universal
1130 Walnut Street, Kansas City, Missouri 64106

www.andrewsmcmeel.com

22 23 24 25 26 RR4 10 9 8 7 6 5 4 3 2 1

ISBN: 978-1-5248-7156-7

Library of Congress Control Number: 2022932543

Editor: Lucas Wetzel
Art Director: Spencer Williams
Production Editor: Jasmine Lim
Production Manager: Chuck Harper

Made by:
Lakeside Book Company
Address and location of manufacturer:
2347 Kratzer Road
Harrisonburg, VA 22802
1st Printing — 8/1/22

Look for these books!

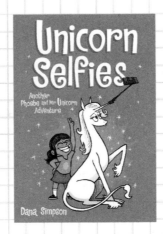